The High-Maintenance Ladies
of the
Zombie Apocalypse

Melinda Marshall

Christine Steendam

Hazelridge Press

ISBN 978-0-9939259-9-3

Published by HAZELRIDGE PRESS

Box 21 Group 37 RR3
Dugald, MB R0E 0K0

Text set in Garamond; Print Edition

Cover design by AP FUCHS
Cover photo by JESSICA GOLLUB
Author photos by JESSICA GOLLUB

M.M.: To John who is partially responsible for creating this high-maintenance lady. Thank you for being so good to me.

C.S.: To Rebekah; a true lady and a total badass.

Table of Contents

Chapter One

Trying New Things is Not Fun

The moment before submersion was the worst.

Vanessa eyed the esthetician crouched before her in a crisp white smock, the woman's bleached-blonde hair gathered into a bun—the texture of steel wool—perched on top of her head. The scent of lavender and aromatic eucalyptus swept over Vanessa.

Vanessa peered down to the tub of clear, steaming water. The water was clean. The tools were clean. At least, that's what they told her. She inquired about their sterilization procedures before agreeing to try out a new spa. Her studies in microbiology made her aware of every last disease that could be contracted from unclean pedicure baths and tools— human papillomavirus, staphylococcus aureus . . .

Miss Bleach Blonde reached a plump hand toward her. "Ma'am, your feet."

Vanessa stared at the hand, at the hyper-orange nails, then at the jetted footbath. Those pipes—*oh, my goodness*. Didn't they know about all the diseases that bred in there, and that there's no way to properly clean them? Maybe she should leave. This was Maddie's idea. Vanessa liked the old place and had never contracted any diseases there. Why did they have to try a new place anyway?

Pressure on her arm drew her attention. "Nessa!" Vanessa drew a breath and looked over at Maddie, her eyebrows raised. "Put your feet in the water."

Vanessa threw Maddie a pleading glance.

Maddie rolled her eyes. "Everything is clean. You're not going to get scabies or salmonella or herpes from the water."

Vanessa opened her mouth to argue, but Maddie continued. "Or flesh-eating disease. Or bubonic plague. Put your feet in the water."

Vanessa nodded in tight motions. "The water, yes. The water." *Don't flip. The water is clean. Act like a normal person.* Vanessa uncurled her toes, aching from clenching them so tight. Miss Bleach Blonde gently took her heels and eased them into the warm water. There was no turning back now. She released a long breath and ran her sweaty palms over her indigo skinny jeans.

Maddie, her feet already in the thick of de-callousing, leaned back in her seat and smiled. Vanessa wanted to relax too but a nagging feeling still lingered. "I feel like something is wrong here."

Maddie smirked. "You feel like something is wrong everywhere."

That was true. "Why couldn't we just stick with the other place? It was so reliable and comfortable and clean and . . . ." Vanessa looked away as the razor blade sliced off the thick skin on her heel. She pressed her eyes closed, and the image of millions of bacteria eating into her skin played in her mind. Vanessa opened her eyes to remove the image and pinned her gaze on Maddie.

Her face smooth, cheeks rosy, Maddie said, "It's fun to try new things."

Another esthetician led a client past them, a woman clutching a fast-food soft drink cup in her manicured hand.

As she passed, the smell of fried food carried to Vanessa. Her stomach growled.

Maddie cocked her head toward Vanessa and said in a loud whisper, "Eww, someone has been hitting McDeath's pretty hard."

Vanessa laughed. She hadn't eaten fast-food in two years, but the smell . . . oh, the smell. So good. But so wrong. Laughing calmed her nerves. She leaned her head back against the headrest, closed her eyes, and this time focused on the sound of rain and twangy instrumental music coming from the speakers above her. She breathed in the hint of lavender scenting the air. Perhaps she could enjoy this after all.

A guttural shout tore through the spa. Vanessa startled, opened her eyes, and peered down the row of pedicure stations. Another shout, low then pitching into a scream.

Six stations down, the woman who'd carried the McDeath cup stood on the seat of her chair. The esthetician reached toward her, but the lady slapped her hand away and shouted a stream of profanities.

Maddie shook her head, staring. "What's her problem?"

Probably doesn't want to put her feet in the bacteria-infested water. "I have no idea. So weird." Vanessa pulled her feet from the warm liquid, the perfect incubation temperature for a host of deadly and disfiguring microbes. Her esthetician didn't seem to notice. She stared, mouth gaping, at the crazed lady.

Other spa clients sniggered then lifted phones, snapped pictures, and took videos. Poor Crazy Lady had been melting down for a grand total of thirty seconds, and she was probably already a Snapchat sensation. Vanessa shook her head and left her phone planted in her pocket.

Crazy Lady picked up her McDeath cup and flung it at the client beside her. The lid popped off and brown liquid and ice exploded from the cup and rained on everyone within a five-foot radius.

Vanessa's gaze bounced between the diseased water and Crazy Lady. This place was a horrible idea. "I think we should go."

Maddie didn't peel her eyes from the screeching woman when she said, "Yeah, maybe."

Another scream filled the air but cut off mid-shriek. Crazy Lady doubled over and gagged.

The esthetician reached for Crazy Lady again. "Ma'am, please." Crazy Lady straightened up, and her eyes widened as though it was a rabid rat moving toward her instead of a hand. "No!" Her shoulders heaved. Her hand flew to her mouth, but vomit exploded out around her palm and between her fingers. Brown and pink chunks and yellowy liquid hit women on both sides of her. She dropped her arm and a gush of puke struck the esthetician. A heaving gag and the esthetician bent over and lost her lunch too. Others groaned and dry heaved.

A warm acid tang drifted on the air. Bile climbed Vanessa's throat. "I'm out." She stood. If they didn't get out of there quickly, they'd all be covered in partially digested food.

Maddie snatched up her purse. "Yeah, me too. Let's go." Maddie rose to her feet as the woman beside Crazy Lady spewed puke into her footbath.

Vanessa attempted to keep her cool, carefully stepping down from the pedicure platform into the aisle, but the moment her feet hit the hardwood, she ran toward the front of the spa. She glanced back to see Maddie trotting behind her.

The receptionist eyed them as they passed her. "What's going on back there?"

Vanessa stopped and shook her head. "If I were you, I'd go home now. There's some sort of stomach flu . . . ." A shiver ran down her back. Was she already exposed? Did Crazy Lady spread her disease to them already?

The receptionist took a step toward the doorway.

"Seriously," Maddie said, hurrying for the coatrack. "Don't."

Vanessa searched for her shoes—the cutest Nine West heels—which she'd tucked away behind the coatrack so no other shoes could touch them. Her foot hovered over the shoe. Her skin was still damp from being in the footbath. The contaminated footbath. Instead, she snagged a couple tissues from the reception desk and wrapped them around her heels before scooping them into her arms.

Vanessa reached for her jacket, hanging on the crowded coatrack. Another garment had been hung over the top of hers. Was it Crazy Lady's? It sort of looked like her size. What if her jacket contaminated Vanessa's? Vanessa drew her hand back. She could just buy a new jacket.

Maddie shrugged into her leather double rider and extracted her long hair from the collar. "Grab your jacket! Let's go."

"Forget it." Vanessa hurried toward the door. Maddie rolled her eyes and flung the door open

"Um, you need to pay," the receptionist called out.

A crisp breeze swirled around Vanessa. "Pay for having you expose me to some unknown disease? I think not."

Vanessa and Maddie hurried outside. Vanessa's feet hit the cold sidewalk, and she lifted her heels to tiptoe. Damn. She spied a patch of blackened gum stuck to the pavement. She chose to look away. Better old gum than vomit, though.

Maddie folded her arms and hurried down the sidewalk. "Damn it. Now my feet feel lopsided."

"We can go back to the old salon, and they can fix you up." That's where they should have gone in the first place. The cool air struck Vanessa's arms, raising goosebumps. She rubbed her arms to warm them.

Vanessa's skin felt thick and heavy. Dirty. Between the cold and the layers of writhing bacteria she was certain covered her, all she could think about was getting home and into a boiling hot shower. With a scrub brush. And soap. And a bleach rinse. She looked down at her blouse and slacks. She might have to burn them.

Thank goodness her shoes were safe.

Chapter Two

You Don't Melt at the Sight of McSteamy

"Maddie, can you run down to X-ray and pick up my reports?" asked Dr. Strong, walking into the reception area from his office.

Maddie's heart rate picked up. She looked up from the computer while clicking to open the scheduling program to hide the fitness blog she'd been reading. That was close. Dr. Strong frowned upon personal items during work hours. She put on her best smile. "Sure. Can I get you anything else while I'm up?" she asked in the sweetest voice she could muster.

"No, that's all for now. But make sure you get those reports sorted before you leave for the day."

Maddie looked at the time on her computer. 4:47. Technically, she could clock out in a little under fifteen minutes, but she'd probably have to stay late to sort the reports. Great. And she didn't even get overtime. "Sure thing."

She pushed back her chair and left the room, head held high, shoulders straight, confidence in her stride. *Walk like you own the world and someday you will.* *Not in this job, I won't.*

Dr. Strong was not exactly who she'd pictured working for when she applied for the position of surgeon's administrative assistant. Tall—at least he had that going for him—fifty or so pounds overweight, and a receding hairline. He wasn't at all the McSteamy Maddie had been hoping for, but the job paid well, too well to pass up. It offered her independence and security without holding her down, and it gave her an in with the other surgeons, and everyone knew that surgeons were high on the list of eligible bachelors. They were practically the MVPs of medicine. Not that settling down with a doctor was on her to-do list, but she certainly wouldn't say no to dating one.

Maddie's heels echoed down the tiled halls as she hurried toward the diagnostic imaging department. Where her office was clean, pristine, and smelled of cinnamon wax melts, out here in the halls, the sterile smell of bleach mixed with the scent of disease made for a noxious mix that assaulted her nostrils. She screwed up her face in distaste and picked up her pace past the ER. After the scene at the nail salon a couple of days ago, she didn't want to spend even a second longer than necessary in the general vicinity of sick people. Whatever it was that was going around, it wasn't pretty.

Despite her rush, muffled conversations still managed to reach her ears. Words like "crazy," "insane," "lost it," and "violent" all seemed to scream out at her from the ER.

She jogged up the hall that ended at the X-ray department. She knocked on the large door a couple times and waited.

"Come on in," came a deep voice.

Maddie pushed open the heavy door—designed to block radiation—and slipped into the dimly-lit room. A man in a white lab coat spun his stool around to face her, and her heart fluttered in response to his welcoming grin. Now this. *This* was McSteamy.

"Hey, Maddie. You need Dr. Strong's reports? Or did you just come to keep me company?"

Heat filled her face. *Come on, pull yourself together. He's just a guy. A really hot guy. But just a guy. Who looks a little like Dean Winchester. But just a guy. Stop. You're a strong woman. You don't melt at the sight of McSteamy.* Oh, but she did. Her knees felt a little weak, and she could feel herself slipping into giggly-teen-girl mode.

"You're funny, Luke, but last I checked I'm not paid to keep a lonely X-ray tech company." *That wasn't bad. Good job.*

"It was worth a shot. It's been so dead here my entire shift. Thank goodness it's almost over."

Maddie frowned. "That's weird. The ER was packed when I walked by this morning, and it still looked busy just now. You'd think you'd be hopping."

Luke pressed his lips together and shrugged. "No broken bones, I guess. There's that weird flu that's been going around. I guess that's what's keeping everyone so busy."

Maddie slipped by him and grabbed Dr. Strong's reports from his cubby. She knocked them against the counter to straighten out the paper and turned back to Luke. "Well, if you're bored, you could walk me back to my office. I wouldn't mind an escort with all the craziness going on."

"I don't blame you. One of the nurses got assaulted this afternoon. Did you hear about that?"

"No, I didn't." Which was strange. She usually knew everything that went on around her wing of the hospital.

"Yeah, some woman went nuts. Started screaming and yelling, and when a nurse tried to calm her down she went ballistic. Someone said she bit the nurse—drew blood and everything. Now she has to get tetanus and rabies shots, the whole shebang."

"Shitty," Maddie said, but her mind went back to the nail salon. What was going on? She'd thought the salon was weird, but the crazy just kept coming.

"I know, right?" Luke got up and slipped off his lab coat and threw it on his stool. Underneath the lab coat, he sported a button-up shirt open enough to reveal the top of a classic rock T-shirt. She liked him like this. He looked less professional, more fun. More let's-go-see–a-concert fun. "Come on, the sooner we get you upstairs to your office, the sooner we can clock out and head home."

Luke opened the door for her, his arm muscles flexing from the effort. He must work out. She should ask him about that, in a non-creepy way, of course. Maybe they could hit up the gym together? She brushed by him, closer than necessary. Had he sucked in a breath there? She pressed her lips together to smother a satisfied smile, but it still tugged at the edges of her lips. The door closed, and they walked side-by-side down the hall. This time, Maddie sauntered rather than rushed, the hospital stench not bothering her, or just not nearly as important as making the minutes with Luke last as long as possible.

"So, any plans tonight? Wednesday and all?"

Maddie looked at him. "Nothing much. Wednesday I go over to my friend's place, and we drink wine and watch TV."

"Oh yeah, what show?"

"*Supernatural*," she replied.

"Can't say I've watched that one."

Strike one. At least he had everything else going for him. "Yeah, we've been watching it since we were in high school. It's become a bit of a tradition."

"Cool."

"Look out!" a voice shouted behind her.

Maddie whipped around in the direction of the warning call. The ER. A couple of security guards chased after a huge man—*huge*—as he barreled out of the ER waiting room and toward her and Luke. She stared at the man charging her. Even though she internally screamed to run, her feet remained glued to the ground. Frozen, she waited to be hit by a freight train.

A tug on her arm un-glued her feet, and she lurched forward and out of the course of collision. Luke threw himself between her and the would-be assailant and pushed her along the hall. She looked back to see a security guard dive and tackle the man to the ground amidst screaming and struggles. More guards ran up, converging around the downed man as he yelled at them.

"Just keep walking," Luke urged her, taking her hand and pulling her along.

They slipped into the stairwell and took the steps two at a time in a rush to get as far away from the scene as possible. Only the harsh sound of her heels hitting tile and the softer whisk of Luke's runners filled the stairway. Not a word passed between them, but Maddie's thoughts screamed so loud in her head she was pretty sure Luke heard them. *Get out! Get out! Get out!*

She burst into her office, tossed the reports on her desk, and grabbed her coat from the closet. She'd sort through them later. Tomorrow. Maybe. If she didn't just call in sick. She really didn't want to come back here.

Luke stood in the doorway, peering down the hall from time to time.

"Do you hear something?" Maddie asked.

He shook his head. "No, just paranoid. That was . . . ."

"Weird?" Maddie asked. "Yeah, and add in the incident earlier today, and my friend and I witnessed something pretty similar at a nail salon over the weekend. It's downright bizarre."

"Look, my shift is over. My replacement should already be downstairs. Why don't I walk you home? You live near here?"

She nodded. "I do, but that's really not necessary." McSteamy walking her home *would* be nice. She'd feel a little safer. Not that she needed a guy to protect her.

"Please. I'll sleep better knowing you're safe." A slight pink hue graced his neck and cheeks, and he looked at his feet, his hand finding its way up to his neck and scratching the back of it.

"All right," Maddie said not nearly as put out as she made it seem.

"I'll just run downstairs and get my stuff. Wait up here, okay? Just . . . lock the door."

Maddie forced out a nervous smile. "Worried about me, Luke?" She meant the words to sound flirtatious, but they came out a little too sincere, a little too real given the circumstances.

He shrugged. "Just a little. You're too pretty to get caught up in the apocalypse."

A laugh escaped her lips. Apocalypse? That seemed like a bit of an overreaction. A flu virus and a couple of insane people hardly meant they were in an apocalypse. "Hurry back, okay? I just wanna get out of here."

Luke nodded and walked out, closing the door behind him. Maddie rushed to the door and locked it, then turned back to her desk and went about shutting down her computer and tidying things up. Grabbing her phone from the desk, she swiped the screen on and pulled up Vanessa's name.

She typed out a quick text describing the near miss with the crazy guy in the hall and finished with letting her know Luke would be walking her home, but almost as soon as she finished writing the text, she erased it. No sense in worrying Vanessa.

Maddie started the text over: *McSteamy is walking me home from work! I'll fill you in later. See you at seven.*

Chapter Three

The Intern Cave

Vanessa's phone buzzed in her lab coat pocket as she squinted into the microscope, counting white blood cells. She needed to verify Nora's experiment results. Why she bothered, she didn't know. Nora, the intern, never made a mistake. Someday, she was certain, it would be Nora who would be verifying *her* results. The only thing worse than a lazy intern was an overly-keen intern, a can-do-my-job-better-than-me intern.

Vanessa had tried sending Nora home multiple times this morning. Nora performed her lab trials between running to the bathroom to vomit, stating she wouldn't let a little stomach issue keep her from her work. She was probably infecting everyone in the lab. Dr. Chalmers went home sick at lunch.

She signed off on Nora's results and folded the file folder closed. She breathed in the quiet of the lab, the subdued whir of the centrifuge the only sound. With that stomach virus going around, she'd secluded herself to a table at the back of the lab. It took every ounce of will she possessed to not wear a surgical mask everywhere she went.

She stripped off her latex gloves, tossed them in the trash, then pulled the phone from her pocket, reluctant to take a look. During lunch, she'd munched on a spinach and quinoa salad and read news report after news report on the illness sweeping the city—the crowded ERs and admonishments to those who were ill to keep hydrated and those who hadn't been struck to frequently wash their hands. Add to the mix an unusual amount of violent assaults, and it made Vanessa want to hold up in her condo, all seven locks engaged. *What's going on in this city?*

After that incident at the spa, she thought for sure she would come down with whatever it was, but she hadn't. Though, stomach viruses had a two-to-seven-day incubation period, and it had only been a couple of days, so she still wasn't out of the woods.

She read Maddie's text and sighed. Of course McSteamy was walking her home. If Vanessa didn't love Maddie so much, she'd hate her. Maddie's luck with men never ceased to amaze her. She was so smooth. Always knew what to say. *Unlike me.* Vanessa had one bit of luck five years ago, but she'd managed to botch it. She shook her head to banish the thought.

Vanessa tucked the folder under her arm and walked to the sink for probably the twentieth time that day. She stepped on the stainless steel pedal to get the hot water flowing and stuck her chapped hands into the scalding liquid. She pumped the soap dispenser three times and then scrubbed, the soap stinging her cracking knuckles and the smell of antiseptic burning her nostrils.

After drying her hands, she walked down the hall to what she and the other researchers called, "The Intern Cave," a small room with no outside windows and a flickering fluorescent light. She peered through the door's window— emblazoned with the MicroScan Pharmaceuticals logo—and into the Intern Cave door.

Nora wasn't at her desk. *Thank goodness.* She wouldn't have to stand beside her and breathe the same air.

The other intern, Graeme, was hunched over his desk, a large book open in front of him. A fast-food paper bag, corners saturated with grease, sat on the corner of his desk.

What a great name. Graeme. Graeme. Graeme. She repeated his name in her head. Her stomach lifted. She tried to force the feeling away. He was only twenty-one, nine years her junior for goodness sake. Too young for her, she told herself. Way too young for her. But she hadn't had a date since . . . when? Five years.

Don't even think about it. But her pulse wasn't listening. She must be desperate.

She twisted the doorknob and pushed, but the door didn't budge. *Damn it.* How many times had they asked maintenance to fix this door? She jiggled the knob and tried again. The door remained stuck, so she knocked on the glass.

Graeme lifted his head, a crease between his eyebrows. A smile brightened his face when he locked eyes with her. She smiled back. It felt like one of those goofy, moony grins, so she pressed her lips together and pointed down at the knob.

He nodded, hurried to the door, and opened it. "Better to get stuck on the outside than the inside of this place," Graeme said with an easy laugh.

Vanessa stepped inside. The salty scent of french fries and ketchup greeted her. She closed the door, and Graeme returned to his desk. He picked up his pencil and resumed his hunched position.

Vanessa glanced around. "Where's Nora?"

Graeme stared down at his papers. "Bathroom. Again."

Vanessa shivered. Why didn't she just go home? She walked to Nora's tidy desk and dropped the file onto the faux wood grain. Graeme scratched something onto a form in front of him. Vanessa took a couple of steps closer and peered over his shoulder at a partially-eaten burger sitting on a paper wrapper and then at a diagram of the male reproductive system. He wrote "vas deferens" on a line connected to a winding tube on the drawing.

Then, her eyes drifted to his tanned neck. She adored that spot where his hair met the skin on his neck. What would it feel like? *Stop looking at him that way. You know this is total cougar behavior, right?*

He turned his head to look back at her. Could he tell she was staring at his neck? *Oh, goodness.* She squared her shoulders and drew a breath to say something but . . . nothing came out. She just stood there, mouth hanging open. Maddie would say something funny and alluring right now. What would she say? *Say something, you idiot!*

She swung her gaze back to the partially-filled-out diagram. "Nice penis."

His brow furrowed. "Huh?"

She went rigid. *Why did I say that?* "I didn't mean . . . *your* penis. Your penis isn't nice. No! I mean . . . I didn't mean your penis isn't nice. I'm sure it's nice. Really nice. Not that I've been looking. I'd never look. Not that I wouldn't like to look." *Shit.* "I'm sure it's nice to look at." Her cheeks burned.

His eyes grew wider with every statement.

"I meant your diagram. You really seem to know about . . . penises . . . ." *Stop talking!* "I just mean you're doing a good job of labeling it." She snapped her mouth shut.

"Um," he said, staring at her. She stared back. He reached into the McDeath bag, pulled out a burger, and offered it to her. "W-want one. I've got an extra."

"Meat?"

He chuckled. "Yeah . . . more meat."

The metal tapping of the doorknob jiggling drew Vanessa's attention. She glanced over her shoulder to see

Nora outside the door. With both hands, she wrenched on the knob, her entire body bobbing up and down.

Vanessa turned away from Graeme, happy for once to see Nora.

Nora pounded her fist on the window and shouted, "Let me in!"

What was with the impatience? Vanessa walked toward the door. Nora looked wrecked, her eyes red-rimmed and bloodshot, and her skin the color of a corpse Vanessa once dissected. The bottom of the door thundered as though Nora were kicking it.

"Open it now!" Nora screeched.

Another step closer and Vanessa hesitated, her hand on the doorknob. Nora drew back her arm and punched the glass. It didn't shatter, but blood oozed from her knuckles.

Vanessa gasped. "Nora, calm down."

Nora clamped her teeth together, and her face contorted with rage. She punched the window again, and blood splattered the glass.

Graeme hurried to her side. "What the hell?"

Vanessa swallowed to wet her dry throat. "Call security." Graeme didn't move, still gawking through the bloody glass at Nora.

Nora punched the window again. A hairline crack traveled through the glass.

"Call security. Now!"

Graeme hurried to his desk and picked up the phone. Vanessa put her hands up in surrender and called through the door, "Everything is going to be okay, Nora. Just calm down. No need to get upset."

Nora screamed, a bone-rattling, eardrum-piercing scream. She took three steps back from the door. Graeme's voice rose in the background as he explained the situation to security.

Nora ran at the door and threw herself into it. The deafening thud echoed around the small room.

Vanessa stumbled back from the door. She glanced over her shoulder at Graeme, her heart pounding. "Tell them to hurry!"

Nora rammed her body into the door again. Her head smacked the glass with a sickening crack, and a spiderweb-like series of fissures developed in the glass. A trail of crimson red flowed down Nora's forehead. She hurled herself at the window again and blood exploded onto the glass, completely obscuring Vanessa's view of her. Another blow and a shard of glass clinked to the tile floor.

Men's voices erupted in the hallway, quiet and low. A scream from Nora. Then, shouted warnings. An urgent shout. Another screech from Nora, but this one seemed strangled.

And then everything fell silent.

Vanessa eased back toward the door, one step at a time. She peered through the hole in the glass. One security guard pressed his knee into Nora's back, fixing a set of handcuffs onto her wrists. The other guard, a bite mark on his forearm glistening with blood, spoke in low tones into the walkie-talkie perched on his shoulder. Nora struggled against him, her neck twisted at a nearly impossible angle.

Vanessa twisted the knob and opened the door a crack. The officer said, "Police are on their way. Please stay put until they get here."

Vanessa closed the door.

A retching sound behind her. She turned to see Graeme vomiting into a trash can. *Oh, no. Not him, too.* She tucked herself into the corner as far from Graeme as she could get.

What seemed like years later, the police and paramedics arrived—only after Graeme vomited so much Vanessa was sure the trash can must be full to the brim.

They had to sedate Nora to remove her. The police questioned Vanessa. They told her she was free to go and then questioned Graeme, though Graeme seemed to be getting sicker by the minute, only able to speak a few words between bouts of vomiting.

She hurried to her lab for gloves, a surgical mask, and a swab. As the officers snapped pictures, she sneaked to a droplet of blood on the floor near the lab door and swabbed it up. She returned to her microscope, smeared the blood on a glass slide, and clamped it into the microscope.

She peered through the lens, expecting to see elevated white blood cell counts consistent with an infection. She ran through the count three times and each time got the same answer. Nora's white cell count wasn't elevated at all.

If this disease wasn't bacterial or viral, what could it be?

Chapter Four

A Little Early in the Evening to be that Sloppy

Maddie nudged her skirt down and wrapped her jacket around her a little tighter in the cool evening air. Though the snow had melted and made way for green grass, the temperatures were still colder than she liked. Oh well, soon enough beach and sun tanning weather would be here.

Sangria weather, she thought with longing. Already, during the day, the sun could get hot enough she almost felt the urge to lie out on her balcony and soak up some of that blessed Vitamin D. Too bad she was locked in an office all day.

A loud bang interrupted her thoughts, and Maddie whipped her head in the direction it came from, half expecting to see the crazed patient from earlier barreling at her again, but it was just the lid of a garbage can dropped by a clumsy restaurant employee.

Don't think about the office, she told herself, thinking back to a couple of days earlier when she'd nearly been run over by a crazed patient. But it had resulted in Luke walking her home and staying at her place for dinner—it was the least she could do after he'd walked out of his way to make sure she made it home safely. She just felt bad she'd had to send him on his way. She'd been *so* tempted to text Vanessa and cancel their

Wine and Winchesters plans. *So tempted.* But no one canceled on Dean Winchester. Not even for McSteamy.

Of course, having to cut their time together short on Wednesday had prompted Luke to ask her out on a real date. He'd taken her out last night—sushi at a nice place in a quieter area of downtown that had been a favorite of hers for years. The date had gone well—really well—and she knew Vanessa would be waiting to hear details.

Glancing over her shoulder a few more times than necessary, Maddie reached for the door and hurried into the entrance of the large apartment building where Vanessa made her home. Maddie dialed the buzz code by memory. She looked around the entrance, shuffling from foot-to-foot, tugged on her short skirt again, and waited for a response.

"Hello?" Vanessa's voice crackled over the intercom.

Does she sound strange? Worried? Maddie shook her head. *Vanessa is always worried about something.* "Hey, it's me."

A grating buzz sounded and Maddie yanked open the heavy glass door, rushing into the safety of the building with a quick staccato tap of her heels. As the door clicked shut a calm passed over her. She felt less exposed—safer—than she did out on the street.

Maddie looked over at the door to the stairway and debated taking them over the elevator. She usually did. Never hurt to get a little extra cardio in, and she'd read in *Vogue*—or maybe it was *Women's Health?*—that stairs were a great way to work the entire body at once. But she was in heels and a short skirt, and she'd be getting plenty of cardio on the dance floor tonight. Besides, Vanessa lived on the sixth floor and that was a trek even without heels.

Taking the elevator up to the sixth floor, the doors opened, and she exited into the warmly-lit hallway decorated in light creams and rich reds.

Stopping outside Vanessa's apartment, she knocked and waited. There was the whisk and clink of the chain sliding off, the heavy clunk of the deadbolt, the quieter clicks of five more locks, then the door opened.

"I'm almost ready, just give me five minutes," Vanessa said, putting an earring in and walking away before Maddie even entered the apartment.

Maddie closed the door behind her, replaced one of the locks and the chain. Her hand hovered over another lock. Vanessa would want her to secure them all, but one *should* be enough, so she left them and sat down on the couch to wait for Vanessa. She pulled out her phone and scrolled through Facebook—so many posts about families, boyfriends, vacations, and complaining about illnesses and the flu. Nothing appealed to her except for vacations. Nothing and no one tied her down, and she liked it that way.

The clicking of Vanessa's heels approached and stopped just inside the living room. "Okay, I'm ready. Where are we going?"

Maddie shoved her phone back inside her clutch and stood up. "Area? It's always good on a Saturday night, and we won't have to wait in line."

Vanessa picked up her small, over-the-shoulder purse and keys from the counter. "Sure. I called a cab a little while ago. It should be here soon."

Locking the apartment behind them, the two of them rode the elevator down to the lobby and awaited their ride. A couple minutes later a cab pulled up outside. The girls climbed in and gave the driver their destination.

"So, how did your date go last night?" Vanessa asked.

Maddie couldn't hold back the smile and the flush of pleasant heat that rose up from her core and filled her. "Amazing. He took me to Wasabis."

"Good choice."

"I know, right? We never seemed to lack for anything to talk about. Luke has a great sense of humor. He's smart, gorgeous, and he's totally into fitness."

"So, when are you seeing him again?"

Maddie smiled even broader. "Tomorrow."

Vanessa raised her eyebrow and twisted her lips in an amused smirk. "And when do I get to meet him?"

"Not until he's thoroughly enamored with me, or I've decided whether or not I'm keeping him around for a while. Whichever comes first."

Vanessa's lips pressed together in a thin line of disapproval. Maddie's "player" attitude was a point of contention, but to her credit, Vanessa didn't say anything.

The cab stopped outside a brightly-lit building with a neon sign.

"I got this," said Maddie. "You wanna get the one home?"

"Sure."

Maddie passed a twenty to the cab driver and waited for her change.

The bass from the nightclub pounded out into the street. A pulsing, steady beat—almost like a heartbeat. Maddie and Vanessa walked over to the empty VIP line.

"Hey, Mark," Maddie greeted the doorman, flipping her long auburn hair over her shoulder and leaning in a little closer than necessary.

"Maddie, Vanessa . . . it's been a while. I was beginning to think you'd moved on."

"Never. You know you're our favorite."

He waved them in, and they walked through the doorway into the dark interior. Lights flashed and the air vibrated all around Maddie from the sheer volume of the music. The girl working the cash desk flashed them a smile and held up the stamp to mark their hands.

"Time to go!" a voice broke through the loud music and a scream of pure rage followed.

Maddie looked over at Vanessa and raised her eyebrows. *A little early in the evening to be that sloppy,* she thought as a couple of bouncers dragged a guy by each arm as he struggled and thrashed about. He didn't look like he was trying to get away, though. He looked more like he was trying to attack the bouncers . . . or anyone else who got close enough to lunge at.

The bouncers dragged him out the door, and it slammed shut behind them. Commotion over, everyone seemed to return to whatever they'd been doing before the scene had interrupted them.

The girl working the door—a familiar face but Maddie didn't know her name—looked pale and a little shaken up. She stamped their hands and offered them a smile. "Have fun," she shouted over the music, but her eyes had a wild, worried look to them.

Ditching their coats at the coat check, they pushed their way through the building crowd to the bar.

"Maddie, Vanessa, what'll it be?" one of the bartenders, Kyle, asked.

"I'll have a screwdriver," said Maddie.

Vanessa crossed her arms. "Same."

"Right away."

He walked off to prepare the drinks, and Maddie leaned on the bar to wait. Vanessa stood beside her, careful not to touch the surface.

Kyle returned with the drinks and slid them across the bar. "Here you are. Wanna start a tab?"

"Please," Maddie answered.

"Hey, dude," a guy interrupted, sidling in between Maddie and Vanessa to lean across the bar.

Really? An "excuse me" would be nice, Maddie thought, catching Vanessa's eye.

"What's up?" asked Kyle.

"Got a band-aid or anything back there? That psycho the bouncers took out scratched me."

"Yeah, sure, hold on."

Maddie picked up her drink and followed Vanessa through the throngs of people toward the crowded dance floor. Sipping at her drink, she started swaying her hips to the music.

"So, this Luke," Vanessa shouted, "think you could get serious about him?"

Maddie took a long sip of her drink and shook her head. "We've been on two dates if you count the time he walked me home. I'm not even considering serious right now. I'm not looking for serious."

"Never say never."

"I'm not saying never. I'm saying I'm not looking for it." The DJ switched songs and "Wannabe" by the Spice Girls blasted over the sound system. Maddie caught Vanessa's eye and started singing the words at the top of her lungs, moving her shoulders, hips, and feet to the beat. Vanessa laughed and joined in, their conversation over.

Maddie lost track of how long they'd been dancing. They'd gotten a couple refills on their drinks, but each song seemed to meld into the next.

Vanessa touched her arm. "I'm gonna go to the bathroom."

Maddie nodded and followed her off the dance floor. The brightly-lit bathroom stung Maddie's eyes, and she blinked a couple of times, accepting Vanessa's drink while her friend used a bathroom stall.

A minute later, she exited and went to the sink to wash her hands.

"Excuse me!" shouted a voice filled with panic. A young girl—couldn't be much older than eighteen—burst into the bathroom, wildly looked around the room, lunged toward an open stall, and puked all over the floor.

Maddie felt her eyes widen. "If you kids can't hold your booze, at least try to make it to the toilet to puke."

Vanessa took her drink from Maddie. "Come on." They rushed out of the bathroom to the sound of more retching from the sick girl.

Chapter Five

The Perfect End to the Perfect Evening

Vanessa held her drink between her fingertips, trying for as little skin contact on the glass as possible. The smell of puke still saturated her nostrils, and she was sure that somehow vomit vapors had lacquered her drink in diseases. As they walked toward the dance floor, she searched for a place to ditch the glass.

She set it on a table then hurried to catch up with Maddie as she dug hand sanitizer from her purse. Sometimes she felt like she walked a fine line between normal and falling into an obsessive compulsive abyss. Maddie glanced back and rolled her eyes as Vanessa flicked the cap of her vanilla-scented sanitizer open. Maddie had always kept her from falling over that edge. *My hands are fine. Be normal.* Vanessa snapped the cap closed and tucked the bottle back into her purse.

They found a spot on the dance floor and joined the jostling crowd. A chest-pounding beat rattled the floor. They moved in time to the music, and a playful grin bloomed on Maddie's face. Vanessa spied a guy, shirt unbuttoned to expose chest hair, dancing up behind Maddie, his eyes pinned on her ass. Every time they came to the club. Every. Time. Some ass ogler took a liking to Maddie. Maddie had spent countless hours at the gym to tone that ass. Vanessa held back a grin. Poor guy. He didn't know what he was in for.

Vanessa leaned toward Maddie. "Ass ogler, twelve o'clock."

Maddie sneaked an over-the-shoulder glance. She looked up at the ceiling, then back to Vanessa. "I don't feel like dealing with this tonight."

Vanessa sniggered. "The usual?"

Maddie conspiratorially raised and lowered her eyebrows. They wrapped their arms around each other.

"Make sure you grab my ass so he can see it," Maddie said.

Vanessa stifled her laughter and gave Maddie's butt an elaborate squeeze. The guy saw it. He had to because his gaze was still nailed to Maddie's backside. The guy stopped, his brow furrowed. They moved their hips, grinding to the beat. They guy peered back at his buddies, shook his head, then spun on his heel and danced back toward his group.

Vanessa burst out laughing. "Mission accomplished." She pulled away.

Maddie doubled over in hysterics. "So, how's my ass?"

Controlling fits of laughter, Vanessa said, "The yoga seems to be doing the trick." Vanessa wiped a happy tear from her cheek. Lights flashed and a familiar face lit up across the dance floor. Graeme. He'd missed a couple days of work with that flu that had been going around. He must've been feeling better.

Vanessa watched him over Maddie's shoulder. He moved toward the ass ogler and his circle of friends. Between flashes of red, green, and yellow light he walked faster and faster, his jaw tight and gaze narrowed. His nostrils flared.

Someone slammed into Vanessa's back and Maddie caught her as she stumbled forward. Vanessa looked back to see the guy who'd asked the bartender for a band-aid hovering over a guy on his hands and knees. The crowd pushed away from him. The sound of retching surged over top of the music. Fluid poured from his mouth and nose.

"Oh, my . . . ." Maddie covered her mouth.

Vanessa grabbed her arm. "Let's get out of—"

A scream tore through the club. Then another. From the other side of the dance floor, people ran toward them, shoving dancers aside. A woman in stiletto heels toppled to the floor as Ass Ogler pushed her out of the way. Terror streaked his features. His hand pressed to his neck, dark liquid covered his shirt and matted his chest hair. Blood! A spurt gushed between his fingers. He stopped, swayed on his feet, then collapsed to his knees. Graeme ran up behind Ass Ogler, his mouth and neck coated in blood. Graeme leaped onto his back and his weight slammed Ass Ogler down, Ogler's head cracking against the floor.

What in the hell? Vanessa stepped forward. "Graeme?"

Graeme clutched handfuls of the guy's hair and smashed the guy's head into the floor with a sickening thud. He bit into the back of his neck and tore away a lump of flesh. Bone glistened under the flashing lights. A pool of blood swelled around them.

Maddie grabbed onto Vanessa. "Come on Nessa!"

Vanessa locked her feet in place. Then louder, "Graeme?"

He lifted his head, eyes wild and bloodshot.

Vanessa stiffened as Graeme released his grip on Ass Ogler. Graeme stood and splashed his shoe in the blood puddle. Then he sprinted for Vanessa.

"Nessa!" Maddie screeched.

They ran for the door, following the panicking crowd. A low growl cut through the screams. Vanessa stole a split-second glance over her shoulder as they plowed between people. Graeme barreled toward them. Only a couple paces behind them, he reached for Vanessa. She struggled to keep up with Maddie and her longer stride. The guy in front of her tripped, and she crashed into him. A yank at her hair pulled her backward. She screamed. Off balance, she hit the floor. Pain rolled up her back, and air bursted out of her lungs.

Graeme jumped toward her, and she threw out her arms to stop him. Blood stained his teeth to a revolting red-orange, darker between each tooth. He wrestled against her, fighting closer and closer to her neck. Maddie's shoes appeared beside her. She kicked and landed a blow to Graeme's temple. He blinked, seeming disoriented. Vanessa shoved him sideways. Another kick and Graeme tumbled off Vanessa. Maddie yanked her to her feet, and they sprinted for the door.

Graeme's guttural shouts followed them. The door wasn't large enough for the number of people trying to escape. People shoved and clawed through the bottleneck. Vanessa and Maddie rammed the crowd, forcing themselves between terrified clubbers. Graeme reached the throng. Just before Vanessa stepped out into the cool night air, he hauled down a security guard twice his size.

Free of the crowd, Vanessa and Maddie ran down the street. They ran two blocks before they slowed down. Tears streamed down Vanessa's face.

"Are you okay?" Maddie asked between heavy breaths.

Vanessa swallowed hard, her throat so dry sound could barely escape. She nodded. "I think so." She looked at her hands and arms where she'd fought off Graeme. No broken skin.

Maddie dialed, then pressed the phone to her ear. She gave their location to the cab company and then stowed her phone in her purse. "They said it should only be a couple minutes."

Vanessa's stomach twisted as images of Graeme flashed in her thoughts.

Maddie touched her back. "Are you sure you're okay? Did he hurt you?"

"I'm okay. Just . . . just shaken up." Graeme. He'd been a friend, someone she would have liked to consider as more than a friend. He wasn't usually violent like that. He was a nice guy. Seeing him like that . . . like Nora that day at the lab. Vanessa froze, and for a moment, she couldn't breathe.

The cab pulled up to the curb. Maddie hurried for the door, opened it, and offered for Vanessa to get in first, but Vanessa stood, locked to the sidewalk. Vanessa stared forward. She didn't see the street or the buildings, no, her mind was at work, the puzzle pieces clicking together brighter than any streetlight or neon sign.

"Nessa? Come on. Let's get you home, okay?" Maddie's voice was a background noise.

A hand on Vanessa's arm roused her. Maddie led her to the cab and guided her inside. With Maddie beside her and directions given to the driver, the car sped forward.

"Nessa, talk to me. What's going on? Do you need to see a doctor?"

Vanessa shook her head. "We need to pack our things. We need to get out of the city." Her voice pitched with anxiety.

Maddie raised her eyebrows so high they touched her bangs. "Leave the city? It was just some guy who went nuts."

"Some guy? That was Graeme from my lab. He's not like that."

Maddie looked out the window, then back to Vanessa. "Maybe he was on a bad trip."

"We need to get out of the city." Her voice quivered.

"Look, that freaked me out too. We'll go back to your place, have a glass of wine, and then we'll feel better."

"You said yourself, there was a crazy at the clinic last week," Vanessa said.

Maddie shrugged. "It's not totally unusual. Sometimes crazies come in. It happens."

"Nora got sick—this stomach thing that's been going around. Then she turned violent. Same thing happened to Graeme. He called in sick the past few days. Now he's turned violent, too."

Maddie tilted her head and quirked her lips. "You think it's some sort of illness?"

Vanessa fidgeted with the hem of her skirt. "After the incident with Nora last week, I ran some tests on some of her blood I found on the floor."

"And?"

"I found nothing unusual."

"Okay, so it's just a couple people losing it."

"When we get home, we need to pack our things. I think the best thing to do is to get as far away from people as we can."

Maddie placed her hand on top of Vanessa's. "You're overreacting. You said you found nothing in the blood work—no weird virus or bacteria."

A tear rolled down Vanessa's cheek. "It could be something much worse."

Maddie wrapped an arm around Vanessa's shoulders. "You said to tell you when you're freaking out. Well, you're freaking out. Everything is going to be okay. I promise. Okay?"

Vanessa drew a trembling breath. "Maddie, I have such a bad feeling. Please. Let's just get out of here."

"I don't have any vacation time left and neither do you and paranoia doesn't count for sick days." She gave Vanessa a squeeze. "Get some sleep. Everything will seem less intense in the morning." She grinned. "Trust me."

Chapter Six

Don't Look Too Excited

Maddie Oed her lips and widened her eyes as she applied thick black mascara to her lashes . . . the finishing touch to her painted-on face.

Luke would be here in a half-hour. The plan had been to go out, but with everything that had been happening lately, Maddie had asked him to change their plans and stay in. She'd told Vanessa everything was fine, that they didn't have to leave the city, that she was being paranoid, but the truth was she didn't believe a word of it.

Last night at the club had been crazy . . . horror movie-esque. The scene of panicked people stampeding out had replayed over and over in her mind, and every time she closed her eyes she was transported back. Sleep had been impossible. She'd managed to go to the gym this morning and go for a run, but it hadn't been the release she'd needed. Instead, she'd spent the entire time studying everyone else in the gym, watching them for signs of violence or illness.

What if Vanessa is right? What if it's something worse?

She closed the tube of mascara and shook her head. No, it wasn't anything uncontainable. It wouldn't be long before they'd get answers, before a name and a cure were applied to whatever this madness was.

After leaving the bathroom, she tidied up around the living room, scooping up fallen throw pillows and folding her couch blanket. Looking around her small, quiet apartment, satisfied with the state of cleanliness, she picked up her phone off the coffee table and checked to see if she had any notifications.

Still twenty minutes to kill before Luke would get here. . . .

Scrolling through Instagram, she double tapped a few pictures and then switched to the camera, snapping a selfie. Studying it, she cringed. Were those crow's-feet around her eyes? Thank goodness for hair dye or her gray hair would show, and that reminded her, she was due to get her roots done. A thin line of dull brown hair was beginning to show against the auburn she'd been rocking lately.

I'm getting old, she thought and clicked through different filters to see which one hid her flaws the best. Satisfied with one, she pressed share and let it join the newsfeed. Putting the phone down, she got up off the couch to check her outfit in the mirror one last time.

Skinny, light blue jeans and a loose-fitted neutral long sleeve shirt; comfortable yet attractive, perfect for a stay-in date. *Maybe I should change* . . . . Her cellphone rang, distracting her from her thoughts, and she hurried back to the living room. "Hello?"

"Hey, I'm downstairs," Luke said, his voice sounding distant and a little tinny through the downstairs intercom.

"Just a second."

She pressed the button to buzz open the door and then set the phone aside to wait the minute or two it would take for him to get to her apartment. Checking her phone, she noticed it was eight on the dot. Punctual. She liked that.

She paced back and forth a couple of times, not sure if she should sit or busy herself doing something until he came.

The solid thump of a knock sounded, and she took a deep breath, smiled, and forced herself to walk at an acceptable pace. *Don't look too excited.* She unlocked the door and removed the chain in a slow and methodical way, then opened the door.

She took Luke in. He looked good. Really good. Of course, he always did. In a hospital environment, people tended to have their bad days—even Maddie had hers—but not Luke. Although, he did look a little pale right now.

"Hey, come on in." She stepped aside to allow him access to her apartment and closed the door behind him.

"I brought some beer and some wine," he said, holding up a paper bag. "I didn't peg you for much of a beer drinker."

And thoughtful. Could he be any more perfect? *Nope. But something has got to give. Nobody is* that *perfect.* She pushed the thought away. "Yeah, beer, not really my thing."

They walked together to the small kitchen, and Maddie dug out a corkscrew. "Do you need an opener?" She offered the bottle opener side of the implement to Luke.

He wrapped his fist around the neck of the beer bottle. "Twist offs." He wrenched the lid off with a pop and a hiss.

"Can I get you anything to eat?" She put some muscle into twisting the corkscrew into the cork.

"I'm good. I had some fast food on the way here."

Maddie grimaced at the thought of the greasy junk food. She couldn't even stand the smell of it much less the taste . . . and such a stupid waste of calories. She'd rather spend those extra calories on frozen yogurt or chocolate *or wine.* She pushed the metal arms down and the cork emerged from the bottle with a pop.

"I hope it's good," Luke said. "I don't really know anything about wine."

Maddie poured herself a glass and smiled. "You did good. This is a really nice red."

"I figured spending a few more bucks meant most choices would be safe."

"Generally."

They walked over to the couch, and Maddie curled her legs up beside her and leaned ever so slightly into Luke's side—not enough to be considered too forward but enough to let him know she was *definitely* attracted to him.

He slipped his arm around her shoulder and pulled her against him. "So, what are we watching?"

Maddie smiled, breathing in his clean scent—soap mixed with pine—with somewhat less pleasant overtones of burgers and fries. He felt sturdy as she leaned into him—solid, unwavering in his confidence and seemingly comfortable to just be with her. Happy little butterflies danced around in her stomach, and she flicked on the TV. "Not sure. We could rent something or just find something on Netflix. What are you in the mood for?"

He shrugged. "I don't really know. Anything except for a chick flick."

"There's this foreign drama I've really been wanting to watch." Maddie smirked.

Luke chuckled. "Okay, not that either, smartass."

She looked up at him, meeting his eyes. They drew her in. Should she kiss him? She really wanted to, but she had a rule—the guy had to make the first move. If he couldn't bring himself to make a move, then he wasn't worth her time.

Please.

He leaned in closer.

He's going to do it! Is my breath okay? Of course it is, I just brushed my teeth. What if he's a bad kisser? What if he's sloppy? The good-looking ones are always the worst. Stop it, Maddie! This is McSteamy, and he's about to kiss me!

His hand found her cheek, and his lips descended on hers. Soft and then more insistent, and her mind emptied of every thought except for, *I hope this never stops.*

Time stood still, and the only thing that mattered was her and Luke and the incredible feeling of his lips on hers.

And then it stopped. He pulled back, his eyes wide, his face paler than it had been a few minutes ago, and he jumped up off the couch and sprinted for the bathroom. The door slammed, and the thin walls allowed her to hear the retching that followed seconds later.

"Was it that bad?" she asked.

She breathed into her hand and sniffed. Mint mixed with wine. It didn't smell unpleasant. Luke had looked a little pale when he'd arrived, but he acted normal so she'd assumed everything was fine.

I'm gonna get the flu. Ugh, just what I need.

She sat on the couch, frozen in place, her thoughts spinning at a hundred miles a minute. The noises from the bathroom stopped, but Luke didn't emerge. Maybe he was embarrassed. She knew she'd be. She got up and walked to the door.

She knocked. "Are you okay?"

A groan came from inside but no words.

"Do you need anything?"

Nothing.

"Luke?"

Panic seized her. What if he'd passed out in there? What if he needed help? He probably had food poisoning after eating that crap that tried to pass for food. She knew she should open the door to check on him, but flashes of the nail salon and then the hospital and then the bar passed through her mind. What if it wasn't something as simple as food poisoning or the flu? What if he had whatever was making people go crazy?

What if Vanessa had been right?

I need to get him out of here.

She tested the doorknob and it turned with ease. He must not have had a chance to lock it. Hesitant and ready to run at a moment's notice, Maddie pulled open the door and peered into the small bathroom. The stench of puke assaulted her nostrils, and she gagged. Covering her nose and mouth with her hand, she knelt down beside Luke. He leaned against the corner of the tub and doorframe, his face a gray pallor, his skin shining with sweat. Yellow bile spotted his chin, and his eyes were glassy and unfocused.

"Luke? I'm going to call you a cab, okay? You need to get home. Do you think you can do that?"

He didn't even groan, just stared as if looking right through her.

She stood up on shaky legs. "I'll be right back." She walked to the living room where she'd left her phone. Picking it up, she scrolled through her contacts to find the cab company she usually used. A dispatcher picked up after only a couple of rings. She gave her address then hung up. It'd only be a couple of minutes. Time to get him moving.

"Maddie?" Luke's voice cut through the silence of the apartment. He sounded strange—empty and cold.

She paused, frozen. "Luke… a cab is on its way to pick you up. Let's go wait downstairs."

She needed to get him out of her apartment. If she could just get him out the door, she could bolt herself in.

"Maddie," he growled.

She shuddered and slowly turned to face him. His bloodshot eyes focused, his jaw clenched and unclenched, and Maddie saw in him the same crazed look she'd seen in the lady at the spa, then the man at the hospital, and then at the bar. Maddie edged backward toward the kitchen. She didn't break eye contact with him. Instinct told her the minute she looked away he'd pounce.

Her hand found the nearly-full bottle of wine. "Luke, why don't you sit down? You're not yourself," she said in a calm, relaxing, even tone. Her voice trembled a little, though, despite her efforts to hide her fear.

She gripped the bottle in one hand, slid it off the counter, and held it low at her side, trying to appear unthreatening. She slipped her phone into her back pocket to free up her other hand then stepped backward along the counter to a drawer and eased it open, careful not to make any sudden movements. She felt around for her butcher knife but kept finding serving spoons. *I need to look.* She took a shuddering breath and tightened her grip on the wine bottle. *One . . . two . . . three . . . .*

She broke eye contact and looked in the drawer. *No!* The knife wasn't there! A growl rumbled from Luke. She looked up. He barreled toward her. She drew her arm back and hurled the bottle at him. Red wine streamed out of the open bottle, splattering over the walls and carpet. The bottle connected with Luke's head with a clunk and then fell to the floor and rolled away. A puddle of red wine expanded around it. Luke shook his head. That should have been enough to knock him out but his eyes burned with animalistic rage, more clear than ever, and every ounce of that rage focused on her. He lunged for her.

Maddie spun away from him, his hands grasping at her shirt. She still smelled the burgers, but the soap and pine scent was now overpowered by the stench of bile. She yanked away; the sound of the material ripping tore through the apartment. Free, she pumped her legs, propelling her to the door at a sprint. She flung the door open and bolted into the hall. Barefoot, she ran for the stairwell and rushed down the stairs.

A loud bang followed by the squeal of the stairwell door spurred her forward. Luke's pounding steps echoed all around her, playing tricks on her ears. She couldn't tell if he was right behind her or a floor behind, and she didn't dare look back to see.

She burst through the door into the lobby. She swore she felt his hot breath on her neck. The heavy metal door slammed shut behind her, and she paused, her hand on the glass door leading outside, and waited. Everything remained silent for just a moment and then a bang, like a gunshot, erupted and the stairwell door shook. Maddie didn't wait around to see if Luke made it through. She pushed open the exterior door and ran out into the cool night air. A block away, she hesitantly stopped and leaned down on her knees to catch her breath. Her eyes darted to every person, every movement, and she looked for signs, that glint in an eye, anything that would act as an early warning she was about to be attacked. *I need to get out of here.*

She took off down the sidewalk at a steady jog, her bare feet slapping against the cold pavement. Vanessa lived only a couple of blocks away. The smell of Luke seemed to float around her, stick to her, follow her, making her think he was right behind her. She kept glancing over her shoulder, and then pushed herself for a little more speed.

Finally, *finally* she pushed through the front door of Vanessa's building and buzzed her apartment. She continued to scan the street outside, stepping from foot to foot, only now realizing how cold they were.

"Hello?" Vanessa said.

"Nessa! Buzz me in!"

The door buzzed open without any questions.

Maddie jammed her thumb against the elevator button and once again took note of her surroundings. Her eyes settled on the stairwell, and she shivered, half-expecting for the door to begin reverberating from an attack. *No. You're safe here. Luke is way back at your building.* Her muscles shook, and she protectively wrapped her arms around her chest.

The elevator dinged, and she leaped into the small metal box and pressed the sixth-floor button and then the one to close the door, continuously pressing it until the doors finally sealed shut. The light for each floor seemed to take forever to flick by. Maddie leaned against the far corner, her eyes darting from the floor indicator to the door and back again. The door opened, and she looked around before stepping out of the elevator. She walked the corridor, her legs trembling. Vanessa's head peered out of her partially-opened door halfway down the hall.

Safe!

Vanessa let her in and pressed the door closed behind her, taking the time to latch all seven locks. Tears of both fear and relief streamed down her cheeks, and she stumbled into Vanessa's arms.

She felt Vanessa guide her to the couch, and she collapsed into the plush cushions.

"What happened?" Vanessa asked.

"Luke . . ." she managed to choke out. "He changed . . . he's . . . a crazy . . . ."

Chapter Seven

A Quiet Evening at Home

Sometimes knowledge was a burden.

Vanessa eyed her phone from her spot on the sofa, then returned her gaze to the muted TV, tuned into a news station. She worked at controlling her breathing. It had calmed, but sensation hadn't returned to her arms. She should take a pill, but she didn't want to. She needed to be alert. She'd spent the morning watching her Facebook and Twitter feeds. So many people ill. So many people reporting encounters with lunatics. And yet, nothing on the news.

She twirled a strand of fringe from her throw blanket around her index finger. From her experience working with infectious disease, she knew the lack of media coverage meant only one of two things—either whatever was going on was so minor it wasn't even newsworthy, or they were withholding information so they didn't create a panic.

"I shouldn't have listened to Maddie," she said. The walls seemed to amplify the words in the otherwise silent apartment. She should have told the cab driver to drive them out of town. In her panicked paranoid moments, she'd made plans, plans to leave the city at the first sign of an epidemic. She'd collected stocks of water and food packed in bins to take with her. She was prepared. How could she have let Maddie talk her out of it?

Her phone rang and she startled. Someone wanted to be buzzed in, but who? She stared at the phone. Maddie was on a date with McSteamy. No one else ever visited—not with her family living so far away. If Maddie got serious with McSteamy, she might even lose her one visitor. No, no! If Maddie found someone, she would be happy for her.

She answered the phone. Maddie's jittery voice slid through the speaker. Vanessa buzzed her in, then unlocked seven locks and opened the door just enough to let Maddie in, her face streaked with tears. She reengaged the locks and turned to face Maddie. What the hell did that bastard do to her?

When Luke's name and the word "crazy" came out of her mouth, Vanessa went cold.

The smell of wine clung to Maddie, little droplets of purple liquid dried on her arms. "Did he hurt you?"

"I-I don't think so." Her breathing hitched. "He just . . . he came after me. He was chasing me." A sob convulsed her.

She glanced at her door and its locks. The locksmith looked at her as if she were unstable when he was installing them, but her paranoia was paying off. There was no way Luke was getting through all that.

She grabbed a box of tissues off the kitchen island and handed them to Maddie. Running mascara blackened her friend's cheeks.

With a quaking hand, Maddie smudged away the tears and the mascara. "Nessa, I think you were right. We need to get out of here. We need to leave. Something bad is happening." Her voice cracked on the final word.

Vanessa breathed out a sigh of relief. She took Maddie's hand and gave it a comforting squeeze. "You stay here tonight just in case Luke is hanging around your apartment.

I'll pack and then we'll go by your place first thing tomorrow morning and get your stuff."

Maddie shook her head in rapid movements. "No, no. I think we should go now." She rubbed the back of her neck.

Vanessa stroked Maddie's back. "It's safer to travel during the day. And don't worry. We'll be safe here for the night." Such a rational answer. Normally, it was Maddie who was the rational one, stroking Vanessa's back when she started to panic. She squared her shoulders at the thought of the role reversal.

Then, a horrific thought swirled in Vanessa's mind—what if Luke had infected Maddie? Vanessa's entire body stiffened. She slid her hand off Maddie's back and stood.

Maddie looked up at her and blinked. "What? What's wrong?"

Vanessa twisted her hands together, and her gaze darted to the pump dispenser of hand sanitizer on the table beside the door. "What did you and Luke do before he got . . . crazy?"

"We had a drink and then . . . ." Maddie's mouth fell open.

"And then?"

"He—oh no—he kissed me."

Vanessa pulled in a sharp breath. No, no, no. Maddie couldn't get this—whatever this was.

Maddie threw her hand over her mouth. "Can I get it that way?"

"I don't know. If it's what I think it is, then no, but I can't be sure."

Maddie stood, five wadded up tissues tumbling to the floor. Vanessa eyed them as though they might slither toward her and attack.

Vanessa pressed her hands together. "Okay, we just need to stay calm and think this through." *Did she really just say that?*

She had to figure this out. She had to be there for Maddie even if it meant exposing herself to this disease. Vanessa shuddered.

Something caught Maddie's attention, and her eyes narrowed. Vanessa followed her stare, peering over her shoulder at the TV. A red bar stretched across the bottom of the screen. Vanessa grabbed the remote and cranked the volume. Alternating high then low tones buzzed from the speakers.

Words streamed along the red band. A voice spoke. "Warning. An infectious outbreak, causing nausea, dizziness, and violent behavior is affecting the city. A quarantine is in effect. All resident are asked to stay indoors and await further instructions. If someone in your home is ill, please phone the emergency hotline." A phone number drifted across the screen.

The remote control slipped from Vanessa's hand and bounced onto the area rug. *It's too late.*

Maddie hauled in a ragged breath. "We can't leave?"

Vanessa nodded. She'd prepared for this—her stockpiles, the locks on the door, the cash she kept stashed under her mattress. "We're going to be okay. I have enough supplies here for two weeks." A lead weight dropped into her stomach. "A week with two of us here." They should have this under control by then, shouldn't they?

Maddie drew another ragged breath. "By then this whole thing should pass, right?"

Vanessa nodded. "Definitely. For sure. Of course it will." She locked eyes with Maddie. If they both agreed on a lie, was it still a lie?

Maddie pressed her lips together. "Hey, maybe this will be fun. Time off work. All the Wine and Winchesters we can handle." She pushed out a nervous laugh that fell flat.

"Dean. All Dean, all the time." Vanessa stretched her lips into a fake smile.

Maddie retrieved the remote from the floor. It trembled with her hand.

Vanessa took a couple steps toward the kitchen. "I'll get the wine." She filled two large wine glasses halfway. Who was she kidding? They'd be drinking more than that. She topped them both up and set them on the coffee table. Vanessa went to the kitchen and returned with a large empty bowl and handed it to Maddie. "Just in case."

Maddie's shoulders drooped. "What if I . . . ."

"You won't!" Vanessa set her lips in a firm line.

Maddie nodded and wedged the bowl between her and the arm of the sofa.

Vanessa settled onto the couch as Maddie pressed play on an episode of *Supernatural*. What would she do if Maddie did get sick . . . or worse, went crazy? She couldn't watch that happen to her best friend.

"Could you turn it up?" Vanessa asked, hoping the noise would drown out the blare of her worries.

Maddie cranked it up, and they sipped wine while Sam and Dean shot salt at demons. Every few minutes, Vanessa glanced over at Maddie, watching for any sign of illness. So far, she looked better than when she arrived. Maybe she would be okay. *Please let her be okay.*

The sun set outside Vanessa's window, and Maddie turned on a lamp while the next episode loaded.

Vanessa shuffled to the kitchen for another bottle of wine. The wine had her feeling relaxed, optimistic even. Maddie would be fine. They'd get through this. It was actually lucky what happened with Luke. If he hadn't gone nuts, Vanessa would be spending the quarantine alone. She popped the cork, returned to the living room, and sloshed some wine into both glasses. She sunk into the sofa and raised her glass. "To Dean."

"To Dean." Maddie tapped her glass against Vanessa's.

A scream carried through the window. Maddie muted the TV. Vanessa walked to the window. In the light of the streetlamp below, a woman screamed again as another woman lunged at her and knocked her to the ground. It looked like she was kissing her neck, but when she drew back, blood blackened her throat. Vanessa stumbled back from the window. Maddie appeared beside her and gasped.

Vanessa scrambled for her phone. She dialed 911 and waited. The low cycling tone of a busy signal droned in her ear. "What the hell?" She ended the call and dropped the phone.

Maddie turned away from the window, all color drained from her face. "What is happening?" she asked, her voice hoarse.

A bang echoed outside the door. Stomping footsteps rattled down the hallway. Vanessa hurried to the door and peeked through the peephole. People ran down the hall. Diagonal to her right, two men kicked at an apartment door. When the door didn't budge, they both threw their shoulders into it. One backed up and ran at the door. He hurled himself against it, and his head crashed against the door. Blood stained the wood, and the door exploded open.

Shouts broke out in the apartment. A scream. Her elderly neighbor ran through the doorway, but one of the men grabbed her hair and slammed her to the ground. He raised his fist and pounded it down at the woman's head.

Vanessa gasped.

"What's going on?" Maddie called from the other side of the room.

Both men's heads whipped up in the direction of Vanessa's door, their eyes bloodshot and wild. Blood peppered their scruffy cheeks. One of the men's eyes narrowed as he zeroed in on the peephole. His murderous stare bore into Vanessa. She stepped back from the door.

A moment later, her door jolted. A thud thundered through the room.

Vanessa scrambled toward the sofa. "Help me move the couch!"

Another boom and another.

They each grabbed an arm of the sofa and slid it over the hardwood floors. The feet ground against the gleaming wood, but Vanessa didn't care anymore about the state of her floors or the condo she'd taken so much pride in.

It was a bunker now.

They shoved it in front of the door as another thud tore through the air. The door groaned with the sound of straining metal. The sofa only covered the lower half of the door. They turned the couch on its arm end, shoved it against the door, and braced their bodies against it. Vanessa's legs burned as she forced her weight against the barricade. Another boom.

Then everything went silent except for their heavy, panting breaths. Vanessa's heartbeat drummed in her ears. Did they give up and go away? She and Maddie exchanged glances, but neither moved.

A choir of guttural shouts behind the door and deafening crashes surrounded them. The sofa jolted forward an inch.

But the door held.

Vanessa waited, muscles tensed for the next onslaught. Maddie pushed, her biceps flexed, against the sofa.

Footfalls pounded down the hall. More banging rang out but not against her door this time. Shouting and screaming vibrated through the walls from the neighboring apartment. She knew her neighbors on that side—a young couple with a new baby. Vanessa wanted to cover her ears, but she had a white-knuckled grip on the sofa that she refused to release. Panicked yells assaulted her ears. The baby cried.

Then both sounds silenced.

Tears burned Vanessa's eyes.

The lights flickered and then cut out, dropping them into terrifying darkness. Faint light from the streetlights below yellowed the window sill. Someone must have cut her building's power.

Vanessa searched through the darkness. There could be crazies in there with them, and they'd never see them. In the corners, faint shadows twisted into enraged crazies, ready to attack.

More shouts. More screams. Farther away now.

Vanessa's arms and legs trembled. Exhaustion collapsed her legs, and she fell to the floor. She leaned her back against the sofa, still butted up against the door. Maddie slid to the floor and scooted over to her. She grabbed hold of Vanessa's hand. Vanessa clung to Maddie's hand as tears streamed down her cheeks.

Chapter Eight

One Day at a Time

. . . The lights flickered and then cut out, dropping them into terrifying darkness.

Maddie tried to even out her breathing. *Everything is okay,* she told herself. *Breathe in… one… two… three… breathe out…* But her pounding heart wouldn't let her. She slid to the floor beside Vanessa. Maddie felt her friend trembling, only feeding her own fear. *The power is out. This is it. No power means no water, no internet. How long before our cell phones die, and we have no contact with the outside world?*

Maddie searched for Vanessa's hand in the dark, for an anchor on reality. She grabbed hold of it and squeezed. Vanessa's hand was clammy with sweat, and it trembled in hers. *She's barely holding it together.*

Maddie took another deep breath, tilted her head back to stare at the dark ceiling, and slowly let it out.

One day at a time.

Day One

Maddie woke up to a loud click and then a buzz. She blinked and then opened her eyes. Her butt was sore, and her neck was stiff. Vanessa leaned against her shoulder, breathing deep, still sleeping.

Maddie stared into the apartment. Lights glowed in the living room and numbers flashed on the microwave. She rolled her head back and forth to loosen up her neck and collect her thoughts. Last night. Luke. Screaming. They'd barricaded the door. The lights. The power was back. The world was quiet now.

If the building could get power back, maybe they had things outside under control?

She touched Vanessa's shoulder. "Nessa. Wake up. The power is back on."

She stirred, then sat up and looked around in confusion. "It's quiet," she muttered.

Maddie nodded and stood, stretching her arms and back. "I'm going to call my mom and see how things are outside of the city. Wanna start coffee?" Maddie couldn't imagine going a day without the dark liquid and the pounding behind her eyes let her know she'd waited longer than usual for that first morning cup.

Vanessa nodded. "You're feeling all right? Normal?"

Maddie nodded. "Exhausted and a little terrified, but yeah, normal."

"Thank goodness." Vanessa got up and walked to the kitchen.

Digging her phone out of her pocket, Maddie scrolled through her contacts to find her parents' number. After pressing the little phone icon, it took a moment for the call to connect and start ringing.

"Hello?" The gravelly baritone of her dad's voice raised goosebumps on her arms.

"Is Mom around?" she asked, not even bothering with niceties.

"I'll get her in a minute. Are you good, Madelyn?"

No one called her Madelyn. Only her dad. The sound of her full name churned her stomach, and for a moment, she regretted making the phone call. "Yeah, I'm good. I just want to talk to Mom."

Her dad huffed, as though he was frustrated, and then he bellowed out, "Michelle! Phone!"

Maddie grimaced and waited for the much quieter, calmer, reassuring voice of her mother. While she waited, she watched Vanessa spray down the counters with a disinfecting cleaner and scrub them with a damp cloth while the coffee brewed.

"Maddie?" Her mom's voice seemed quieter than usual, almost a whisper, or maybe it was just Maddie's imagination running away on her.

"Mom, how are you? How is everything out there?"

When her parents moved north of the city to a secluded acreage, Maddie had refused to go along. Only seventeen, she'd taken whatever job she could find to pay rent in whatever dump apartment she could afford. Anything to get away from her dad. She only visited at Christmas, and she only called on her mom's birthday. It wasn't that she didn't love her mom; she just couldn't worry about her. Michelle Connor had chosen her path, and Maddie couldn't walk it with her.

"Things are good out here. Quiet. We've seen the news, though. Are you and Vanessa all right?"

Maddie smiled at her mom's concern. Michelle Connor never seemed to hold Maddie's leaving against her. Sometimes Maddie thought she even envied her freedom. "We're both okay. We're together at Vanessa's condo, and we've got plenty of supplies to hold us over until this is all done. What about you? You have enough to eat?"

"Oh yes. We have tons of canned goods from my garden last year and a fully-stocked freezer and cold storage. We'd have enough supplies for the Apocalypse."

"Good. And Dad? He's been treating you okay?"

"Oh, Maddie, don't be so hard on your dad. He's a good man."

"He's a mean man, Mom."

"He's a good man, Maddie. He just likes things a certain way. I wish you'd talk to him. He loves you, and this grudge you're holding hurts him."

"The way *he* treats *you* hurts *me*."

"He treats me just fine. You're not giving him a chance, Maddie. You're just looking at him through the paint you brushed on him when you were a moody teenager."

Maddie drew in a deep breath until her lungs tightened then slowly let it out. There was no point in arguing. She'd had this discussion countless times. It was part of the reason why she rarely called. "Okay, Mom. Just, call if you need anything. Tell Dad I said goodbye."

"I'll tell him you love him."

Maddie closed her eyes. "All right, Mom. I love you. Bye."

She hung up and lowered the phone to the floor beside her. Her hand left the warm plastic of the phone and ran through the tangled mess of her hair. Looking over at Vanessa, she saw her friend had paused her morning cleaning ritual and their eyes met. Vanessa offered a half-hearted smile, but her eyes gleamed with a sympathy Maddie didn't want. It didn't matter. None of it mattered. She'd left that life twelve years ago. She couldn't let it get her down now.

Day Two

Curling up on the floor in a nest of blankets and pillows beside Vanessa, Maddie handed her friend a glass of wine. "Okay, start the episode."

They'd been binge watching *Supernatural* since yesterday morning. Starting back at the very beginning at season one episode one and continuing from there.

Vanessa pressed play on episode one of season two and the haunting tones of "Carry on My Wayward Son" filled the apartment as the season recap played.

Maddie took a sip of wine. "What do you think Dean would do in this situation?"

"Kick ass." Vanessa grinned. "He wouldn't be holed up in an apartment, that's for sure."

"He'd be out there slaying crazies and wooing women." Maddie sighed. "Think he'd woo us if he were here?"

Vanessa giggled. "Oh, definitely. But Dean is totally mine. You can have Sam."

Maddie rolled her eyes. How many times had they had this argument? "We share him. Come on, that was the plan."

Vanessa shrugged. "We'll see."

"Well, if you're going to play it like that, I guess I'll just have to keep him to myself."

Vanessa looked down at her lap and pressed her lips together. "Yeah, 'cause he'd go for you first."

It was supposed to be sarcastic, Maddie knew that, but a hint of sadness tinged Vanessa's words. Maddie wished Vanessa could be more confident, could believe more in herself, her brilliance, her capabilities, her beauty.

"He'd probably end up dead at some point, though," Maddie said, trying to take the focus off of the two of them.

Vanessa stared at the blanket for a long silent moment. "Except in Dean's world, dead is never really dead . . ." she whispered.

Maddie shivered at the thought and focused on the TV. *Don't think about it. Don't think about it. We're just having a girl's week with Wine and Winchesters.*

Day Three
"Maddie, read this."

Maddie set down her phone—Instagram was pretty boring lately anyway—and accepted Vanessa's. A blog post. Vanessa liked bloggers. She said they were today's journalists and the only ones not controlled by big corporations.

Maddie read the headline: "The Apocalypse is Here, and the Government is Lying to Us."

"Seriously, Vanessa? This is just fearmongering. Don't read this crap. My mom said things are quiet in the country. If the Apocalypse was here that wouldn't be the case."

"Read the article. Just read it. The writer makes some really good points."

"It's all conspiracy theories. I'm not buying into this." She handed the phone back to Vanessa without reading further and picked hers back up, switching to Facebook and scrolling through the newsfeeds. "Huh."

Vanessa cranked her neck to peek at Maddie's screen. "What?"

"You remember Grant Baker?"

"From high school?"

"Yeah. Apparently his wife got hit by a car."

"Is she okay?"

Maddie shook her head. "She's dead."

She met Vanessa's eyes. Neither said anything. Maddie didn't say the words she could see in Vanessa's gaze. *More crazies?*

Day Four

"You know what I miss?" asked Maddie, rolling over onto her stomach. The hot noonday sun beat down on her, and the world seemed oddly quiet for midweek downtown. They laid on Vanessa's balcony soaking up some sun.

"The beach?"

Maddie reached for her glass of sangria they'd whipped up from a few of Vanessa's supplies and took a sip. "Yes, but I was gonna say dancing."

Vanessa looked at her and grimaced. "I don't know if I ever want to go dancing again after what happened last time."

"You can't dwell on that. It's just some weird flu virus going around or something. A freak moment. Are you going to avoid the nail salon and the hospital, too?"

"You know I hate those things, so I already did, when you'd let me."

Maddie laughed. "I'm not going to let you avoid dancing. Come on." She turned the music up on her phone and stood, swaying her hips and putting her hands in the air.

Vanessa's eye-roll didn't go unnoticed, but Maddie laughed and grabbed her friend's hands, pulling her to her feet. As they danced, Maddie felt the stress and worry melt away, and a smile began to creep onto Vanessa's face. Had she seen Nessa smile even once since she'd arrived at her apartment four days ago?

Day Five

"Now take a deep breath and move into Warrior three," the TV instructed.

Maddie and Vanessa followed the directions with practiced ease. Normally, they had Friday morning yoga class at their gym, but since the quarantine, they'd decided to just use a yoga DVD Vanessa had lying around collecting dust.

"Now go into Tree Pose then begin your Sun Salutation."

Yoga cleared Maddie's mind and leveled her emotions in a way no other exercise could. Exactly what she needed after being cooped up in an apartment for five days straight.

"Namaste," the video concluded.

"Namaste," Maddie said.

Vanessa didn't repeat it, though. She never did. She just walked off to the bathroom and started the shower.

Okay, then, thought Maddie. If she didn't know Nessa so well, she'd wonder if she was mad. But she knew her friend, and she knew she just needed some alone time. That's fine. It meant she could enjoy her coffee in silence.

She waited for the kettle to come to a boil and then added the water to the glass beaker filled with coffee grinds. Setting the timer on her phone, she waited for the coffee to steep. *Does coffee steep?* She scrolled through her Instagram feed.

The timer beeped, and she pushed down the plunger of the French press. Maddie poured herself a cup and breathed in the scent. Coffee and wine were the two things she absolutely could not do without. The minute the black nectar of wakefulness and sweet juice of joy ran out, she knew things would get bad.

Day Six

Vanessa popped the cork on a bottle of red, poured a glass, and slid it across the counter to Maddie. "This is the last bottle."

"Guess we better savor it."

"I have a box." Vanessa shrugged.

Maddie grimaced. "Boxed wine? Ugh, I'm not sure I can drink that."

"Beggars can't be choosers."

"I choose to think we'll get out of this place before I need to stoop to drinking boxed wine."

Day Seven

Maddie groaned and lay down on the floor.

"What's wrong?" Vanessa asked from the kitchen where she prepared breakfast. Maddie didn't have to look up to hear the panic in her voice.

She groaned again and pressed the palm of her hand into her lower stomach. "Cramps."

"Cramp-cramps? Or sick cramps?" Vanessa's voice squeaked out.

Maddie rolled her eyes. "Cramp-cramps."

"I have some Midol in the cupboard." Vanessa grabbed the plastic bottle out of the cupboard, opened it, and delivered the pill along with a bottle of water to Maddie.

Maddie reached up and accepted them. "Is coffee ready yet?"

"A couple more minutes."

Maddie sighed and sat up, throwing the pill into the back of her mouth and swallowing it. "Okay, I'll be right back."

She walked into the bathroom and opened the drawer in the vanity where Vanessa kept the feminine products. This wasn't the first time she'd needed to borrow a tampon from her best friend. She grabbed the box and sat down on the toilet. Looking inside, her heart stopped, and she was suddenly nauseated. There was only one left.

It's okay. Vanessa has a week's worth of supplies. Surely she has tampons.

She removed the wrapper from the tampon and finished up. Walking back out into the main living area, she went straight to the kitchen and the waiting French press and poured herself a big, steaming mug of black coffee. Vanessa sat in the nest. She looked at her phone, likely scrolling through social media or reading blog posts—the conspiracy theory ones that drove Maddie crazy, but mostly because they terrified her and because they fed Vanessa's anxiety and neurotic tendencies.

"By the way, we're out of tampons in the bathroom. Where do you keep the emergency supplies?" Maddie sipped her coffee. Mmm, hot and strong, just the way she liked it.

Nessa lowered her phone and looked at her, eyes wide. "I don't have any."

"What do you mean?"

"I mean, I didn't think of including them in my emergency supply list."

Maddie closed her eyes and took a deep breath. *It's okay. It's okay.* "It's okay," she said. "We'll just have to go on a supply run."

Chapter Nine

Should have Stocked up on Certain Essentials

Vanessa marched to the bathroom. Maybe she had some tampons tucked away in a drawer. Or maybe they'd fallen out at the back of the cabinet. Perhaps she had a couple maxi pads kicking around.

She always had a box of tampons on hand. Her supply stash covered her for two weeks. That's what the government emergency preparedness websites recommended. With a maximum of one period in two weeks, one box should've been all she needed. She hadn't considered the eventuality of having to share her supplies—or nearly-synchronized periods.

Maddie's suggestion of a supply run was out of the question. According to every TV channel, radio station, and online media outlet, the quarantine was still on. In fact, the quarantine warning was all that was on. Repeated over and over. There hadn't been a live news anchor or radio personality in a couple of days. What did that mean? And what was going on outside?

Vanessa opened each and every drawer, searching their organized contents—trays of nail polish, baskets of make-up, tiny bins of oral hygiene products. No tampons.

Footsteps behind her. She glanced over her shoulder as Maddie folded her arms and leaned against the doorjamb. "I looked everywhere."

Vanessa crouched and opened the cabinet under the sink, scanning the sink's dark underbelly, past bottles of hair product and around pipes. "I just wanted to make sure . . . ." Still no crinkly pink or yellow wrappers. *Damn it.* She reefed open a sealed plastic container labeled "Samples." Foil pouches of shampoo and lotions shimmered up at her. Vanessa pushed them aside. Below, she spied a small square box with a coupon stamped on the side. She victoriously drew it from the container and held it up as though she'd dug the Holy Grail out of her bathroom cabinet. "Found one!"

Maddie's eyebrows bunched up. "Found what?"

"An extra absorbent maxi pad."

Maddie stared at her, lips pressed together.

"With wings!" Vanessa smiled.

Maddie shook her head. "No. Just. No."

"It's better than nothing."

"Really? Would you use that?"

She was right. The very idea of wearing a pad—the feeling. Ew. The smell. Vanessa sighed. They were running low on wine, and they'd been eating canned fruit. Canned fruit! Even the can declared it had zero nutrient value. What she wouldn't give for a kiwi or freshly-squeezed pomegranate juice. But a supply run with that disease running rampant . . . .

"You may be right," Vanessa said. "We're almost out of supplies. But . . . ."

Maddie pushed off the doorway. "Let's get a move on. This tampon is only going to last so long."

Vanessa stood. Her heart thrummed as she considered disengaging the locks on her condo door. What happened out there a week ago vividly flashed in her thoughts. She'd been tempted to move the couch so she could peer through the peephole, but she couldn't bring herself to do it. In some ways, it all seemed surreal. Did she really see what she thought she saw? It felt a lot like a realistic nightmare.

Vanessa closed the cupboard doors. "We need a plan."

"A plan? We walk the three blocks to the drug store and walk home."

Vanessa fidgeted with the hem of her sleeve. "We don't know what it's like out there."

"No one has been on the streets in days." Wide-eyed horror washed over Maddie's face. "Crap! What if stores are closed?"

"I'm sure drug stores will be open. There has to be some sort of infrastructure in place. I'm more worried about the crazies, though."

"Yeah, maybe we should take . . . something just in case."

Vanessa nodded. "I have a baseball bat under my bed. And I have some cash in case debit machines aren't working."

Maddie nodded. "Let's get ready to go then."

They stood in Vanessa's walk-in closet, staring at the racks of clothes and shoes. Having fled her house with nothing but the clothes on her back, Maddie had to borrow from her. Maddie shoved hangers across the bar and finally settled on a pair of fashionably-worn jeans and a teal halter top. Being the shorter of the two, the pants were too short for Maddie, so she rolled them up.

Vanessa lifted her eyebrows. "Nice! I have the perfect shoes to go with that outfit." Vanessa turned her rotating shoe rack, scanning as she went. She grabbed a pair of tangerine sling-back heels.

Maddie's eyes gleamed. "Ooh, I haven't seen these before."

Vanessa grinned. "I just got them. Ordered them in."

Maddie pushed and wiggled her feet into the shoes. Vanessa cringed. Maddie's feet were wider than hers. Vanessa chewed on her cheek. She'd stretch them out. But, this was her best friend, and she'd do anything for her, even ruin a pair Christian Louboutin heels. Her chest ached. "They look great on you!" Vanessa swallowed the lump in her throat.

Maddie furrowed her brow. "Maybe I should just wear some running shoes. Just in case."

"Running shoes? With that outfit? It would be all wrong."

Maddie quirked her lips. "True. I'd need a totally different outfit."

"Besides, my running shoes are at the gym."

"Really? You only have heels?"

Vanessa laughed. "You know how I feel about stunning footwear. Fashion first."

"You know what? We've been cooped up here for a week. May as well look good when we go out." Maddie flashed her a playful smile.

Vanessa chose a pencil skirt and sheer ivory chemise that she pulled over a lime sorbet-colored tank top. She added her silver Steve Madden stilettos. They straightened each other's hair, and carefully applied their make-up. Vanessa made Maddie use cotton swabs and forbade her from double-dipping in her eye make-up. It was for Maddie's own protection. Vanessa still wasn't convinced Maddie wouldn't contract the disease after kissing McSteamy. More like McCreepy. It had been almost a week, but she knew nothing about this disease's incubation period.

While Maddie finished applying her lipstick, Vanessa went to her bed and fished around underneath for the baseball bat. She pulled it out and went for the cash under her mattress.

She swept her hand around until her fingers grazed an envelope. She grabbed hold of a corner and pulled it out. A blue envelope? She'd tucked her cash in a manila envelope. She gasped as five-year-old memories bowled over her.

She skimmed her fingers over the envelope. It had been years since she looked inside. She'd forbidden herself from looking at it, yet she couldn't bear to get rid of it. Like she'd gotten rid of the handwritten notes he'd sent her. Like she'd gotten rid of the ring.

She slid her fingernail under the envelope flap. *Don't look at it. You know how you'll feel when you look at it.* But, she couldn't stop herself. She needed to see it. Just once. She tugged the photo from the pouch. Her breath caught.

Ethan had snapped a selfie. Vanessa had been trying to hide her face in the crook of his neck, but she was laughing. And he was smiling. Every sensation rushed back to her—his scent, the warmth of his neck on her nose, his arm around her.

He'd printed the picture and framed it for her. He'd said he could see her essence in that picture. That thing he couldn't put his finger on that he loved about her. A warm ache tightened her chest.

"You ready?" Maddie's voice rang out from the other side of the bed.

Vanessa shoved the photo back inside the envelope, then back under the mattress. She pushed her hand farther in, located the cash stash, and yanked it toward her. "Um. Yeah. Just getting some cash."

Maddie leaned over the bed. "Something wrong?"

Vanessa blinked away moisture gathered at the corners of her eyes. "No, no. I-I couldn't find the envelope at first."

Maddie's eyes narrowed. "You look upset."

"I'm fine. Just worried about going out, that's all."

Maddie slid onto the bed and crossed her legs. "You sure?"

"Very. Grab the hand sanitizer." Vanessa forced a smile and held up her wad of twenties. "Let's get you some tampons."

Vanessa and Maddie scooted the sofa away from the entrance and set it on its legs. They stood, staring at the door for a long moment. Vanessa gripped the baseball bat.

"I think maybe I should have a weapon too," Maddie said.

"There's a tennis racquet in the entryway closet."

Maddie retrieved the racquet, and then Vanessa eased closer to the door. Would there be a body out there? She couldn't smell anything, but maybe the door blocked the odor. She lifted up on tiptoe and peered through the peephole, bracing herself. Through the fish-eye lens, the hallway stretched in either direction. She scanned right then left. Empty. She saved looking down for last. She pressed her hands against the cool, metal-clad door and let her gaze drop downward. She released a sigh. Blood stained the short paisley carpeting, but there was no body.

Vanessa stepped back from the door. "All clear."

She peered back at Maddie. Her face had lost all color except for what she'd painted on. Maddie nodded. "No problem then, right?"

"Right."

Maddie gripped the racquet tighter. "Run down to the store, get some supplies, run back. No big."

"No big." A nervous giggle escaped Vanessa's lips. Her pulse sped. Her bracelets clattering against each other as

Vanessa, one by one, disengaged the locks—the locks that had saved both of their lives. With each click of a mechanism, Vanessa's heart sped all the more. Her hand on the final bolt, she swallowed against her dry throat. "Get ready." She twisted the lock and it clunked open.

Maddie lifted her racquet, holding it in a white-knuckled grip. Vanessa slowly peeled the door open, her ears tuned to every sound. She stuck her head into the hall and looked both ways. Black stains on the carpet. An acrid smell. Silent and empty. She motioned for Maddie to follow. They stepped into the hallway, weapons perched at their shoulders. They crept down the hall, their stilettos brushing the carpet the only sound besides their breathing.

At the stainless steel elevator doors, Vanessa pushed the blood-encrusted call button with her elbow. She glanced back at the bloodstained carpet while the elevator dinged through floors. What happened to the bodies?

The elevator chimed, and the door slid open. Maddie cranked her neck to check out all the angles of the metal box. They stepped inside, and Vanessa pressed the lobby button with her elbow again. She pulled in a deep breath. "I need some hand sanitizer."

"You haven't touched anything."

Vanessa clenched her teeth. "I. Just. Need. It."

Maddie snatched it out of her handbag and squeezed a pool of sanitizer onto Vanessa's waiting palms. Vanessa scrubbed her hands together. The stinging scent of alcohol covered the musky smell of old blood. Vanessa's breathing evened out. She could do this. Everything was going to be okay.

The elevator ticked downward. What would they find when they reached the lobby? Vanessa thought back to that night a week ago when everything went sideways. Where did the body in the hallway go? Did someone move it? And why hadn't there been any updates online or on TV? They couldn't be the only ones running low on supplies.

The elevator slowed then stopped. Vanessa lifted her bat as the doors slid open.

Maddie pressed her hand against the doors to hold them open and peeked out. "Oh my . . . ." She stepped out of the elevator, and Vanessa followed.

The lobby was devoid of people, but evidence of them clung to every surface. Blood splatter coated the floor-to-ceiling mirrors on the far wall. It stained the carpet. Flies buzzed around a lump of something meaty with long hair protruding from one side.

Vanessa sucked in a breath and held it. Her ears rang. "Maddie. This is a bad idea."

Maddie's eyebrows bunched together, and she looked back at Vanessa. "We only have another day's worth of food. What are we going to do then?" She glanced around her. "Whatever happened here likely happened last week. Maybe it's all over."

"Maybe." But what if it wasn't?

Maddie continued. "We've not seen a soul in days."

If whatever it was had passed, why hadn't there been an all-clear broadcast of some sort? "Still, we need to be on guard."

Maddie's gaze ran over the lobby, then back to Vanessa. "Hell yeah."

Vanessa backed her way out of the red-streaked glass lobby doors and onto the sidewalk. Though she didn't touch the doors, she still demanded sanitizer. Maddie delivered.

They walked the empty sidewalk toward the drug store. Cars sat abandoned on the road, doors hanging open, glass shattered. Dried blood formed violent puddles on the street and sidewalk. With that much blood, people had to have died. But no bodies. The wind whipped past them. It rustled tree branches, but that was the only sound. A city of three-quarters of a million people and the only sound was the wind, the tapping of Vanessa's and Maddie's heels on the pavement, and Vanessa's throbbing heart. No car engines, no horns, no conversations.

Maddie gripped her racquet tighter. "This is eerie. Where did everyone go?"

Vanessa swallowed hard. "I don't know."

Chapter Ten

I Think I Killed Him

Maddie tried to keep her eyes focused in front of her. *Don't look around,* she kept telling herself, but it was as if her eyes were drawn to the most violent scenes—blood splattered across buildings, windows, and the ground, sitting in stagnant, brown puddles buzzing with flies that made it appear alive. Broken glass littered the street and crunched underfoot. She'd stepped into a world of nightmares, and maybe if she'd just pinch herself, she'd wake up.

This was a bad idea, she thought. They never should have left Vanessa's apartment . . . and in heels with only a baseball bat and a tennis racquet for protection? What were they thinking? They needed guns. Scratch that. She had no idea how to shoot one, much less load it, but knives could do a fair bit of damage… against whomever. What would a tennis racket do? And heels? Looking fabulous was one thing, but what if they had to run? She'd had to run from Luke.

"There's the drug store. How do you wanna do this?" asked Vanessa, breaking into Maddie's thoughts.

"Go in together. Everything bad happens in the movies when people separate."

"This isn't the movies, Maddie."

Maddie looked around her. "I know, but it kind of feels like we're in an episode of *Supernatural*, doesn't it?"

Vanessa's silence was answer enough.

Maddie held up her tennis racquet to, what? Hit some crazy in the head? "Do you want to open the door?"

Vanessa looked at the door handle and scrunched up her face. "No way am I touching that. Besides, I have the baseball bat."

Sigh. "Fine, I'll do it. Get ready for . . . ." What? Did either of them really know what to expect?

Vanessa paled, but Maddie had to hand it to her, she didn't back out. She set her feet, clenched her jaw, and stood ready.

Maddie grabbed the handle and pulled. The stench hit her first—the putrid smell of rot mixed with the copper of blood and the grating buzzing of hundreds, if not thousands, of flies. A burning sensation struck her as bile rose up her throat. She swallowed it back, covering her face and mouth with her free hand and motioning with her head for Vanessa to go in.

She looked at Maddie with wide eyes, not a word passing between them, her hand covering her mouth and nose. She hesitated a minute, then walked in, bat still held over her shoulder and ready to strike at anything that moved.

Maddie followed close behind, glancing around the drug store. The store was too big to take in all at once, so they'd have to remain diligent and move fast. Get in, get out. "This way," she said, grabbing a basket and going straight toward the hanging sign that said "Feminine Products"—priority number one. Food could come after. It's not like a drug store had a huge supply of the fresh, organic fruits and vegetables that her diet usually consisted of.

She could almost feel Vanessa's shifty glances, scared and hesitant. Maddie gave up on holding her hand over her mouth. It's not like the barrier did anything to filter the particles in the air. It was more a placebo than anything, and she needed her hand for more important things like collecting supplies.

She stopped in front of the tampons. "Which brand do you like?"

Vanessa shrugged. "These?" She grabbed a random box.

"Those have the stupid cardboard applicators, though. I prefer the plastic."

"Then get the plastic. Why did you ask?"

"In case you had a preference."

"Just grab what you want and let's keep moving," Vanessa snapped.

Sorry for trying to be considerate. Maddie grabbed a box of tampons decorated in bright colors and promising things like comfort and total protection, tossed them in the basket, and then grabbed another. Better to be safe than sorry. "What next?"

"Let's just get some food and go home."

Maddie followed Vanessa toward the sparse food aisle. It didn't look too picked-over. People must have been listening to the quarantine for the most part, which seemed strange since there was no way everyone in the downtown area was as prepared as Vanessa, and even the two of them were running low on food. She glanced over the array of boxed, packaged, and canned foods. Just standing there, she could almost feel herself losing her perfectly toned thighs and abs she'd worked so hard for, but food was food and soon enough the city would get things under control and she could, once again, get her diet—and stomach—under control.

They grabbed canned food off the shelves without really looking at what they were taking. Vanessa took the lead and rushed through the store, filling up the basket. Vanessa, taking the lead—that seemed like such a strange thought. In all their years of friendship, Maddie had always been the leader.

Vanessa rushed around one aisle to the next, the clip of her heels echoing in the seemingly abandoned store.

"Slow down a bit!" Maddie said. "I'm lugging—"

Vanessa's scream tore through the store followed by a hard thwap and the sound of something squishing. It reminded Maddie of the time she had accidentally dropped a watermelon while walking up the stairs to her apartment. Maddie dropped the basket and ran around the corner on the borrowed, un-broken-in heels. Vanessa stood breathing heavy with blood splattered over her once pristine clothing. A gray, partially-bloated body lay at her feet.

"Are you okay?" The smell hit her first and stopped her dead in her tracks beside Vanessa to look at the body, its head indented and leaking. That must have been the watermelon sound. Her stomach clenched and bile burned the back of her throat. She swallowed it. Maddie looked at Vanessa. Tears streamed down Vanessa's face, and she shook her head. "I think I killed him," she whispered.

Maddie knelt down to look a little closer. "I don't know. He looks like he's been dead for a while."

"No, I walked right into him. He was standing, shuffling around. He had to have been alive."

Maddie looked at the body again, the pallor of the skin and, oh goodness, the smell that leeched off of him. There was no way this guy was alive two minutes ago. Absolutely no way. "Maybe he was leaning against the shelf, and you just imagined that he moved?"

Vanessa glowered. "I know what I saw."

Maddie shook her head. "Okay, okay." There was no point in getting Vanessa more upset than she already was. It was probably just fear getting to her, making her imagine things that weren't there. Not a big deal. "Let's finish up here and get home."

She walked back to the basket, spilled on its side, cans of food splayed around the floor. She gathered up the supplies and picked up the basket. "Let's go."

"Water bottles?"

Maddie looked back to the aisle they'd just come from. The aisle with the dead body. "Take this, I'll get it." She shoved the basket of supplies at Vanessa and jogged toward the water, the staccato clip, clip, clip, of her heels making her uneasy. It sounded like a freaking homing beacon for crazies. She paused at the body, shivered, then carried on. Grabbing a case of water, she jogged back. *Thank goodness I've been jogging with weights.*

"Let's go," she said, passing Vanessa.

"We have to pay."

Maddie shook her head. "Who the hell cares?"

"Maddie—"

"No, let's go."

Chapter Eleven

Selfie Time

Vanessa chewed her lip as she stood at the front of the store, clinging to her supply-laden basket. No one was at the cashier's counter. Should they just take the stuff? They couldn't do that. But, Vanessa hadn't been keeping track of prices and then there were taxes to add on. She didn't want to go back and figure out how much the stuff cost. She wanted to get out of here and get back home to her locked door.

What had happened to that guy she ran into? He was standing. He was moving. Yet, she had to agree with Maddie—he looked like he'd been dead for a long time. Maybe it was just a sick combination of fear and imagination making her see things.

She set the basket on the check-out counter and estimated the cost of their supplies.

Maddie leaned toward her. "What are you doing? We need to get out of here."

Vanessa multiplied out the tax, then dug through her purse and extracted a stack of bills. "I'm paying." If they were caught on the surveillance camera, they'd see she at least tried to pay.

"Let's just go." Maddie grabbed the cart handle.

"I'm not stealing this stuff!" Vanessa reached across the counter for a bag.

Maddie groaned and grabbed a bag. "Fine. You pay. I'll bag."

Vanessa counted out her twenties. "Shit. I don't have exact change." She unzipped her change purse to search for some coins. She didn't want to underpay, but she didn't want to overpay either.

"What the hell?" Maddie stopped, a can of peas in her hand. "Is that Tori Bell?"

Vanessa looked up from her collection of loose change.

A woman lumbered toward them, her pale face pocked with scabs, but still recognizable. She wore business attire—gray skirt, navy blazer, white blouse, a pair of frumpy gray pumps. But dirt smeared the skirt and the hem hung unfurled on one side. One of the lapels on her blazer was torn off. Black stains sullied her untucked blouse. One of her heels was ripped off, giving her a Quasimodo-like gait. What a fashion nightmare!

Maddie whispered. "That's Tori Bell from high school, right?"

"Looks like her."

"She looks awful," Maddie said.

Vanessa looked her up and down. "Those shoes look like something my grandmother would wear. And they're broken. What happened to her?"

"Ew." Maddie wrinkled her nose. "She was such a bitch in high school."

"Ew," Vanessa said. "Queen of all bitches."

Tori's cloudy eyes locked on Maddie.

"Shit, she saw me." Maddie waved. "Hey, Tori."

Tori shuffled toward them.

"Oh, my! Why'd you wave?" Vanessa nudged her. "I don't want to talk to her. She looks majorly hungover."

"Yeah, she looks like crap." Maddie shook her head. "What was I supposed to do? She saw me. And maybe she's heard what's going on here."

"She looks too hungover to know anything." But, it was worth a try. Vanessa waved too. "Hey, Tori."

Tori's expression didn't change—no flash of recognition, no return of greeting.

Maddie rolled her eyes. "Same Tori. Stuck-up."

Tori grunted and reached her hands toward Vanessa and Maddie.

"What the hell is wrong with her?" Maddie whispered.

Vanessa tucked the last box of tampons into a bag. "Maybe she's sick. She looks sick."

"But, she's not acting all crazy."

Tori lumbered closer. A large green glob of snot slithered out of her nose.

"Gah, there's something wrong with her." Vanessa swallowed hard.

Maddie covered her mouth. "That's disgusting. Tori Bell green snot." She sniggered. She dug her phone out of her back pocket and clicked through the screens until she found selfie mode. "Get in here." She motioned to Vanessa.

Vanessa leaned in, leaving just enough room between their grinning faces to perfectly frame Tori. Maddie snapped selfies as Tori stumble-stepped closer. Tori's eyes widened and a long moan escaped her throat. She wiggled her fingers toward Maddie's hair.

Maddie stowed her phone and stepped away from her. She and Vanessa both grabbed their bags of supplies. Tori changed direction and lurched toward Maddie again.

A foul smell rolled over Vanessa. She'd thought the smell in the store was bad, but Tori brought things to a whole new level. She smelled like that dead disease-infested mouse she'd found in the trap under her refrigerator. Hot rot, oily and damp. Vanessa's stomach clenched.

Maddie gagged. "Oh, my—" She draped the bags over her arms and returned her hand to her mouth. Tori swiped her arm at Maddie and grabbed her hair. Tori's milky eyes went wild. She opened her mouth wide, exposing yellowed and broken teeth, and tugged Maddie toward her.

Maddie screeched and grabbed the hand curled around a thick wad of her hair. "Get her off!" She swung the tennis racquet and tagged Tori in the knee, but Tori held tight. She took another whack. Tori didn't seem to notice as she pulled Maddie toward her.

Vanessa dropped her bags. "Let go!" Vanessa raised her bat and brought it down on Tori's shoulder. A thud and a pop and Tori lurched forward but her grip refused to loosen.

She threw down the bat then pried at Tori's fingers. Tori snapped her teeth together and pulled Maddie nearer.

Maddie screamed as the teeth clicked closer and closer. "Help me!"

"I'm trying!" Vanessa dug her fingernails into Tori's hand and a chunk of flesh peeled off Tori's finger. Bone shone beneath nearly-black blood.

Stars swam across Vanessa's vision. She stared at the chunk of flesh on her fingers. Her ears rang.

"Nessa!" Maddie hit Tori with the racquet again. It popped out of her hand and fell to the floor.

Maddie's shout sounded distant. Vanessa blinked. Maddie needed her. She drew a deep breath and blinked hard. Vanessa stumbled sideways, dropping the putrid piece of Tori's finger.

Scissors! She needed scissors.

Vanessa sprinted down an aisle where she'd vaguely recalled seeing office supplies. She stopped in front of a display of pens and index cards. "Scissors. Come on!" She grabbed a pair of children's scissors, ripped the package open, and sprinted back to the front of the store.

Tori was noshing on Maddie's hair, blackened drool pouring from her mouth.

Maddie's voice shot high. "She's drooling in my hair!"

Vanessa put the scissors to Maddie's hair. "Hold still!"

"No! No! Don't cut my hair!"

"I have to! There's no other way!"

Tori shoved more of Maddie's hair into her mouth.

"My hair!" She pushed Vanessa away with her foot. "You're not a hairdresser!"

"I'll be careful." Vanessa thrust the scissors down and the blades ground as they chomped through each stranded of Maddie's hair. She opened and closed the scissors over and over, severing more and more of Maddie's beautiful auburn hair. Voices from the back of the store drew her attention.

Two men and a woman, their shirts darkened with blood, appeared at the end of the aisle. Their gazes bore into Vanessa for one long moment.

"Oh, no," Vanessa whispered.

Maddie, pushing against Tori, said, "Hurry!"

The three figures bolted toward them, pushing each other out of the way. One of the men crashed into a display of hand lotion and tumbled to the floor. The other two kept going, scrambling toward them.

Vanessa squeezed the small scissors and cut through the last strands. Maddie fell forward onto the industrial tiles. Vanessa scooped up as many grocery bags as she could with one hand and Maddie's arm with the other. Maddie grabbed the bat as Vanessa yanked her up. Feet thundered toward them.

They ran for the exit, grocery bags banging against Vanessa's thigh. They flew through the door and onto the street. Wind whipped her hair as Vanessa glanced over her shoulder. The woman smashed into a glass panel beside the door. Blood sprayed from her flattened nose. The final man shoved the glass door open so hard it hit the brick exterior and shattered.

They sprinted down the street, but the man was gaining. Another storefront with a steel-clad door lay ahead of them. "There," Vanessa yelled between gasping breaths.

They lunged sideways, and the door swung open. They fell inside, Vanessa's shoulder smacking the concrete floor. A shock of pain rolled over her. Vanessa shoved the door closed with her feet. A loud thud rang out from the door. It budged, and Maddie braced her legs against it. Another deafening thud.

Vanessa's pulse raced, her legs burned, and pain cut into her shoulder as they held the door closed while the man threw his weight against the barrier over and over again.

If he managed to get through, they were done.

Chapter Twelve

Bitch, I Can Run in Anything

Finally, the banging stopped and the world once again returned to silence. Maddie looked over at Vanessa and hesitantly reached up to touch her hair. "How bad is it?"

"Not too bad." Vanessa's voice shot up a note or two at the end. She was lying. It must look horrible.

"It's hacked, isn't it? You hacked it off?"

Vanessa shrugged. "A hairdresser can fix it. Shorter hair is really in these days."

"A hairdresser? Where do you suggest we find a hairdresser to fix my hair? This is pretty much the freaking Apocalypse. Everyone is either hiding or dead or . . . whatever the hell the rest of those *creatures* are. As if getting an emergency hair appointment isn't hard enough, this is pretty much impossible." Maddie knew she was being insane. The last thing she should be worried about was her hacked hair. Vanessa had saved her from Tori—a thought that never would have crossed her mind back in high school. What would have happened if she hadn't been fast enough to think of grabbing scissors and cutting her hair? *Hacking. She hacked.*

Vanessa's eyes went hard. "Some thanks for saving your life, this is. Seriously, Maddie? Screw your hair. Screw your tampons. Screw your freaking health food. No one gives a shit. You keep insisting this isn't anything serious. You don't take me seriously. You refuse to read the news—"

"Conspiracy blogs."

"Shut up! This is exactly what I'm talking about. You can't take anything seriously. You just brush off everything. I killed a guy back there, and you just think I'm crazy. I save you, and all you can think about is your damn hair."

Maddie leaned against the door beside Vanessa and listened to her rant. Her ears rang, and her blood boiled, and she wanted nothing more than to slap her friend and tell her she was scared out of her mind, too. But slapping wouldn't help anything, and it was easier to concentrate on the simple things that helped keep her world normal, like social media and tampons, and, stupid as it was, her hair.

She turned her head to look at Vanessa. She saw the anger and determination in her friend by the way she set her jaw and her eyes straight ahead. "I'm sorry," Maddie whispered.

Vanessa frowned, and her face relaxed a little. "What?"

"I'm sorry. You're right. I'm not taking anything seriously. It's not because I'm not scared. It's because I'm terrified, and it's easier to deal with little things than the prospect we might be the only ones left."

"Well . . ."

"Well?"

"We should go back to the apartment."

Maddie nodded. "Best idea I've heard all day. I could use a bathroom anyway."

They stood and looked at the door.

"Think it's clear?" Vanessa asked.

Maddie shrugged. "It's quiet, but who knows?" Maddie glanced at the bags on the floor beside them. "We should have grabbed a backpack."

"We were in a hurry."

"On three?"

Vanessa nodded and went to pick up the groceries, but as she moved her arm she gasped, and her free hand sprung to her shoulder, clutching it.

Maddie studied her. "Are you all right? Did one of those . . . *things* . . . get you?"

Vanessa shook her head. "I landed funny on my shoulder." She removed her good hand from the shoulder, and Maddie inspected it, not touching, just looking. It seemed to be in an odd spot compared to her other shoulder. "Think you popped it out of place?"

"Could be. Either way, I won't be doing much with this arm."

Maddie's mind spun. They needed to get back to the condo. She tightened her grip on the bat. "You open the door with your good hand, and I'll man the bat, okay?"

Vanessa nodded. "Transfer all the important supplies into a couple bags. I'll open the door, you make sure everything is all clear, and then I'll carry all the supplies I can."

Maddie smiled. "Look at you, all badass, Nessa. I never would have thought I'd see the day."

"I know, right? We've totally got this."

"One..."

Vanessa's hand went to the knob.

"Two..."

She met Maddie's eyes and nodded.

"Three."

Nessa pulled the door open, and Maddie stepped into the doorway, bat held high and ready to swing. The silent world instantly erupted into groans, moans, and other disgusting guttural sounds from a sea of gray, white, green and scabby faces. As far as Maddie could see, faces met hers and not one looked . . . human. Humanoid, sure. But human? Definitely not.

"Get back!" screamed Vanessa.

Maddie lunged backward, and Vanessa slammed the door. They pressed their backs up against it.

"What now?" Maddie asked as a loud bang caused the door to jolt against them.

Vanessa cried out in pain.

Maddie couldn't stand seeing her friend in pain. She pressed her feet into the floor and her shoulders against the door to try to take the brunt of the force.

Pain twisted Vanessa's features.

"We're not going to be able to hold it," Maddie said.

"We have to try."

The door jerked again, and Maddie knew Vanessa was right. "Maybe there's another way out."

"If we move away from this door they'll stream in."

The door bounced forward, opening a crack. Maddie's foot slipped, and she stepped back, trying to regain her balance, but fell against the door, slamming it shut.

Vanessa dropped the bags and cans of peas rolled across the floor. "We could run."

"How are you supposed to run with your shoulder like that? And there's no guarantee there's actually another exit."

"I can do it. I'll suck up the pain. Don't all buildings need multiple exits?"

This time, the force that hit the door didn't let up as if the hoard worked together to push it open. Maddie's feet slid along the floor, her heels squealing in protest.

"I hope so because it might be our only option." Maddie slipped out of the heels and planted her feet. "Kick yours off."

Vanessa shook her head. "No way. Do you know how much these shoes cost?"

Maddie looked down at her friend's feet. They *were* pretty fabulous. "Can you run in them?"

Vanessa smiled, and her gaze narrowed. "Bitch, I can run in anything."

"Good." She reached for the nearest bag, dragged it over, and pulled out the box of tampons. "Let's go."

They let go of the door. Maddie sprang into a run, her bare feet slapping against the concrete floor. The door opened with a bang followed by a chorus of groans, growls, and moans. Thundering of dozens of feet chased them. They'd left all the food behind; it would slow them down too much, but she clung to the box of tampons as her arms swung with every motion of her pumping legs.

For the first time, Maddie was thankful for all those hours spent at the gym, and not because of her figure or because she could fit into some *fine* clothes, but because, damn, she could outrun these fuckers.

Vanessa kept stride right beside her, holding her arm and shoulder tightly against her body, the metronome of the points of her heels slamming against the concrete keeping time. Maddie couldn't help but have a newfound sense of admiration and respect for Nessa. She'd always thought she was the strong one, but she wasn't sure she'd be pushing through the pain like Nessa was.

They rounded a corner in the warehouse, pounding footsteps echoing all around them. Maybe there were crazies in here? They could be hiding anywhere. Blood splattered a wall to Maddie's right, but she didn't have time to investigate further. She looked away and kept running.

They rounded another corner and ran smack into a barricade of desks, chairs, and various boxes. A body lay at the base of the barricade, face stretched out in a permanent expression of pain and terror. Maddie couldn't even tell if it had been male or female. It was missing an arm and the legs lay at unnatural angles. Chunks of flesh were missing from all over, exposing bone and muscle. Maddie couldn't look away, she couldn't turn, she couldn't even stop herself from throwing up her breakfast all over the floor in front of her. They needed an exit, and they needed one now. Finally, she tore her eyes away and looked around.

Nessa's breathing came in wheezy, painful gasps. "What now?"

"Other way."

They ran back the way they came only to come to a skidding halt in front of a bloated, gray, scabby, oozy, *disgusting* looking man wearing a security uniform. He lumbered forward down the middle of the hallway.

"He should lay off the donuts," whispered Maddie, trying not to disturb him by creating any loud noises.

"Or McDeath."

"Yeah, or that."

"We're still trapped," Vanessa said, bringing Maddie back into the here and now.

"We can probably just slip by. He looks slow."

Vanessa raised her eyebrows. "Tori was slow, too. I saw a left turn back there that we passed. We can go that way if we can get by him."

Maddie gripped her box of tampons a little tighter. If they got out of here with anything—besides their lives, of course—it had to be the tampons.

Maddie went first, tiptoeing by the obese security guard. His eyes followed her movement, and he began to lumber toward her instead of Vanessa and the barricade.

"Come on," Maddie hissed, motioning.

Vanessa looked from her to the guard and back again. She started moving forward, the clipping of her heels drawing the guard's attention. She paused, eyes wide.

"Come on!" Maddie hissed again, a little louder. The growls of the horde grew closer. "We need to go!"

Vanessa moved forward again and her heels clipped a few more times. The security guard groaned and lurched forward, stumbling into Vanessa and knocking her to the floor.

"Nessa!" Maddie screamed at the same time a shriek of pain tore out of Vanessa's throat.

Maddie grabbed at the guard's shirt, trying to pull him off. Vanessa, laying on her back, kicked at him. Her shoes connected but it made no impact. All Maddie could do was hold him back from diving in with his gnashing teeth.

Vanessa slammed her foot into the guard's groin. He bellowed and reared up, knocking Maddie away. She scrambled to her feet and grabbed hold of his shoulder just as Vanessa's heel connected with the guard's stomach. His eyes widened and the rest of his face seemed to pucker up. Vanessa's shoe and foot disappeared into his belly. Maddie froze and looked at the guard. Everyone seemed perfectly still, and then a pop, much like a hiss of air followed by an explosion of fluid, burst over them. Maddie turned away, closing her eyes and mouth. Funky, oily liquid drench through her clothes and she groaned.

"Ewwww!" She used a dry section of her shirt to wipe off her face.

Vanessa scrambled out from under the deflated guard draped across her. "Hand sanitizer!" That was the Vanessa she knew.

The stench rolling off of them in noxious waves.

Maddie looked up, wiping bodily fluids off her arms, and stopped. "Oh shit."

"What?"

Maddie pointed at the horde just in front of them.

Chapter Thirteen

You Can Learn Anything on YouTube

Vanessa pressed her lips together as a dribble of slime slid down her face. Putrid goo weighed down her hair and coated her skin. Vanessa breathed in through her nose and the sharp stench made her gag. Bits and pieces of the interior of the security guard—what looked like partially decomposed internal organs—clung to her arms, to Maddie's face, and littered the floor. Thick brown and yellowy liquid dripped from Maddie's elbows.

Guttural screeches rocketed Vanessa from her disgust. She searched around for a place to run, a place to hide. Nothing. They were at a dead end with crazies sprinting toward them. Stepping through the puddle of decay at her feet, she grabbed hold of Maddie.

Maddie embraced her in return. "Goodbye, Nessa."

"Goodbye, Maddie. Love you."

The rabid hoard pushed into the room—an undulating mass of flesh. Vanessa closed her eyes, her pulse throbbing, and waited for the pain—the first dig of fingernails and teeth into her flesh. Would they kill her and Maddie, or would they turn them into crazies too?

The demented voices cut into her ears. Rustling of fabric. Pounding of feet. Bodies brushing against her.

But . . . no pain.

Vanessa carefully opened one eye, then the other. The crazies milled around them like frenetic Christmas shoppers. Their bloodshot eyes darted and searched as they snapped their teeth together. It was almost as though they couldn't see her and Maddie standing right in front of them. Pain boiled in Vanessa's shoulder as she stood stock still, barely daring a breath.

Maddie whispered in her ear, "What's happening?"

Vanessa wanted to shake her head, but couldn't risk the movement. How was it they weren't attacking? She gripped Maddie's arm tighter and slime gushed between her fingers. Could it be because they were covered in the stench of death? Was scent what guided the crazies?

One way to find out. Vanessa eased her mouth closer to Maddie's ear. "Very slowly, we'll back toward the door."

Still locked in each other's arms, Vanessa and Maddie slowly and silently shuffled away from the mass. They bumped into a crazy and nudged it out of the way. It stepped aside and stumbled into another one of its kind. Inch by inch, they made their way to the door.

They released each other, and Vanessa peeled the door open with her good arm. Maddie peeked out at the street then motioned Vanessa after her. They stepped out of the building onto the sidewalk.

Maddie doubled over. Vanessa's legs collapsed out from under her. She grabbed her shoulder as she fell onto the concrete and a shock of agony rolled over her. She tucked her head between her knees. She breathed in and out, every breath a fresh reminder of the filth and disease that covered her.

Maddie's hand skimmed her back. "You okay?"

Vanessa swallowed her forming tears and nodded. "I think so. Except . . . my shoulder."

"Come on. We need to get back to your apartment before we run into any more of those things."

Vanessa nodded again and allowed Maddie to pull her to her feet. Holding her bad arm against her chest, Vanessa said, "I think we need to get out of the city. There could be thousands of those things around."

"I think you're right. Let's head back, pack up, and get as far away from here as we can."

They burst through Vanessa's condo door. Maddie worked the locks for Vanessa who, cradling her arm, went to the kitchen cupboard where she kept pain reliever. Releasing her bad arm to a shot of pain, Vanessa rifled through the cabinet and pulled out a bottle of Ibuprofen. She lifted the lid with her thumb and shook three pills into her mouth and swallowed them dry.

After the seventh lock clicked into place, Maddie appeared at her side. "Let me see."

Vanessa took a deep breath. "I think it's dislocated." Maddie reached out for her, but Vanessa stepped away. "And it hurts like hell."

"Just let me take a look."

"I need a doctor." Vanessa's voice trembled.

"These types of injuries came into Dr. Strong's office all the time. I even watched him reset one once."

Vanessa glared. "Oh, okay. I guess that totally qualifies you to fix this. What was I thinking?"

Maddie pressed her lips into a hard line. "You really want to go back out there and hope the hospital isn't full of crazies like everywhere else has been?"

"Just let me . . . ." Maddie tried reaching for Vanessa again, but Vanessa jerked away, wincing. "What other option do you have?" She released an exasperated sigh. "I let you butcher my hair."

"Oh my goodness, seriously? That's so not the same. Don't compare my dislocated shoulder to your hair . . . that will grow back!"

Maddie bristled and hooked her hand on her hip. "You have a better plan?"

Vanessa peered down at the floor, then at the door. "Gah! No."

"Sit down, and I'll pop it back in."

Vanessa walked to her breakfast nook and pulled a chair away from the table. "You sure you remember how?"

"I-I think so." Maddie's forehead wrinkled.

Vanessa raised her eyebrows. "You *think* so?"

Maddie pulled her phone from her pocket. "There's gotta be a YouTube video—just to give me a refresher."

"You know if you do this wrong, I could lose my arm."

Maddie's mouth fell open. "Really?"

"Yeah, really. No pressure."

Maddie glowered at her and then typed something into her phone. "Sit down."

A male voice issued from her phone speakers, explaining the Kocher's method of relocating a dislocated shoulder. Maddie watched, nodding along. "Okay, are you ready?"

Vanessa swallowed hard and nodded. Her pulse throbbed in her ears as Maddie gently took her bad arm. Even the gentle touch plucked a jab of pain. Vanessa took a couple cleansing breaths. "Okay, do it quick."

Maddie pulled Vanessa's hand away from her body, and Vanessa pressed her eyes closed and clamped her teeth together as agony gripped her. Maddie rotated her arm outward . . . and then in. A pop and a bolt of white hot pain flashed through her entire body. Vanessa screeched as her arm slid back into place.

She opened her eyes to Maddie's pale face. "You did it."

Maddie nodded. "That sounded so . . . so gross." A sweaty sheen glossed her forehead. "You need a sling." She walked toward Vanessa's bedroom.

Vanessa sat, trembling, waiting for her return. Maddie actually did it.

A minute later, she returned with one of Vanessa's scarves, the ends tied together. She draped it around Vanessa's neck and then helped position her arm.

The pain ebbing, Vanessa said, "Thank you."

Maddie nodded. "Anything for my best friend. But, don't ever make me do that again." She flashed a weak smile.

They took turns showering, trying to wash off the stench of death, but it clung to them even after soaping and scrubbing. They packed two backpacks with the essentials—toothbrushes, eye-liner, a change of clothes, a couple of knives, moisturizer, tampons, and what was left of Vanessa's food stocks. With sunset approaching, they decided they'd spend the night in the condo then set out first thing in the morning.

Getting out of the city seemed like the best plan, but Vanessa couldn't help but wonder how many more of the crazies they'd encounter before they made it past the city limits. At least she knew how to hide from them now, not that she cared to repeat the experience.

Vanessa double-checked the locks on her door and climbed into bed beside Maddie, who was already asleep. A dull ache thrummed in her shoulder as she reached her good arm under her mattress and drew out the picture of Ethan.

Was he still alive?

Vanessa's phone vibrated. She hit snooze and stared at the ceiling, enjoying the quiet and what could possibly be her last moments in her own bed. When the phone buzzed again, she dismissed the alarm, then stroked Maddie's shoulder. "We need to get going."

Maddie groaned and opened her eyes. "Are you sure it's the right thing to do . . . to leave here?"

Vanessa had the same doubt. She felt safe here with all her locks, but they'd have to go for supplies again. They couldn't just hang out in the condo forever. "I really don't know if it's the right thing. I've just always read that in the case of an epidemic, it's best to get away from population."

Maddie sighed and peeled herself out of bed. Her shoulder stiff, Vanessa groaned as she followed her. They ate and then dressed, this time in jeans and T-shirts with hoodies over top. They chose practical shoes—Maddie a pair of bronze strappies with two-inch heels and Vanessa, a casual pair of wedge heels. She shoved her silver Steve Maddens into her backpack. She couldn't bear to leave them behind. It would be like leaving your dog behind.

Vanessa positioned her arm in the sling, and then they shrugged into their packs. Vanessa took one last look around her condo—this place was hers. She bought it on her own. It was a symbol of her success and independence.

And security.

Now she had to leave it behind.

She looked over at Maddie. "Ready?"

Maddie nodded, and Vanessa disengaged all the locks. They stepped out of the condo and closed the door.

Chapter Fourteen

This Had Better be the Apocalypse

Even after seeing the blood and gore outside a few times, it still shocked and terrified Maddie when they walked out of Vanessa's apartment for what was probably the last time. All of their possessions—gone. All the shoes and clothes and beautiful things—gone.

"This had better be the Apocalypse, or I'm going to be royally pissed," she whispered to Vanessa.

Vanessa just shook her head and continued walking. Obviously she didn't want to discuss this.

"Which way are we going?" she asked, unnerved by the silence.

That made Vanessa pause. "We should go north."

Maddie's stomach churned. "Why north?" She knew full well she wouldn't like the answer.

"We can head to your parents' place." Vanessa's words were quiet, almost a whisper.

"Absolutely not."

"Please, Maddie. Your mom said it was still safe up there and that they had tons of supplies. They're self-sufficient. We know we'll have shelter, and it won't just be us against the world. Please?"

Maddie hated that pleading look in Vanessa's eyes. She knew going to her parents would be the logical choice, the smart choice, but she just couldn't. She'd worked so hard for her independence. She'd worked so hard to get away from her dad. No way was she about to run to him and give him a reason to control her again. If she did, and they got past all this, he'd hold it over her head—that he helped them, and she owed him. "I'm sorry, Nessa. I just can't. There has to be a different option."

Vanessa sighed. "Then I think we should go east. If you're absolutely against going to your parents—"

"I am. Let's go."

She pulled at the shoulder straps on her backpack—loaded with the majority of the supplies they had left—and continued on alongside her friend. The bright sunlight of the day was a cheery contrast to Maddie's inner heaviness. This wasn't how life was supposed to happen. Walking through a major-city-turned-ghost-town just felt wrong. They shouldn't be the survivors. They were just a couple of city girls. Girls like them never survived. And yet, here they were, the only two people walking the streets.

Groans and growls made up the soundtrack of their hike when they passed dark alleys or shadowed places. *Maybe they don't really like the sun . . . .*

No, they'd chased them out in the sunlight yesterday. So maybe they just rested in dark places.

Her toe hitting something and a tin clattering down the street brought Maddie out of her introspection and back to reality.

"Careful!" hissed Vanessa, stopping to look at her, her eyes accusing.

"I'm sorry."

A growl resonated from the alley to Maddie's left. Two crazies barreled down the alley toward them.

Maddie took off eastward up the street. "Run!" The instant the word left her lips, she realized her mistake. More crazies streamed out from nooks and crannies around buildings or smashed up against glass doors and storefronts. The growls and screeches grew louder and closer. Maddie pumped her legs harder, the impact of her feet hitting the concrete sending vibrations up her legs.

The smell of rot grew stronger and made it hard to breathe without choking on the contaminated air.

"The car!" Vanessa yelled, lurching to the right side of the road to a small parked car.

Maddie didn't hesitate to follow her friend's lead. They had to barricade somewhere; there was no way they'd outrun this horde, and the noise from the crazies would only draw more of them this way.

She pulled at the handle of the backseat on the driver's side and prayed whoever had parked it had forgotten to lock it. The handle responded and the door swung open. She dove inside and pulled it shut behind her. Vanessa scrambled into the driver's seat and slammed the door just as a crazy smashed up against the car at a dead run.

Maddie screamed and slammed down the lock, then scooted backward to the far side of the car.

"Start it!" she yelled at Vanessa, the crazy snarling, gnashing, and drooling on the window.

"I don't know how."

Maddie looked at her. "You know how to drive."

"It's a stick."

"What?"

"It's a stick. I can't drive a stick."

Maddie's body melted into the backseat, and she stared at the crazies surrounding the car, attacking the metal body and rocking the thing back and forth like one of those carnival rides. If they kept it up, she might puke. "I can't drive stick either."

Both went silent. Maddie's heart fell into her stomach, and she sat there, still, quiet, given-up. The same despair emanated off Vanessa and fed her own. This was it, this was how they went. Trapped in a car that would soon enough give way under pressure just because they couldn't start the damn thing.

I can't go out like this. In a shitty Ford hatchback with my hair mangled. I just can't.

"Are there keys?" Maddie asked, dropping her backpack off her shoulders and leaning over the center console.

"Yeah, I guess the owner left in a hurry."

"Okay, then we can figure this out. Move over."

Vanessa climbed to the passenger seat and Maddie shimmied over the console and into the driver's.

Maddie set her jaw and inspected everything. Her hand went to the ignition. She turned the key, and the car sputtered to life, lurched forward, and died. It didn't sound very promising.

"It doesn't work?" Vanessa's high-pitched voice barely contained her panic.

"Just a second." Maddie thought back to her driving lessons. It'd been so long since she'd driven a standard. Or tried, rather. After a brief shouting match with her dad about her inability to follow directions, she'd refused any further help. "Um, YouTube it. There has to be some kind of instructional video on there for this kind of thing."

Vanessa pulled out her phone. The rocking of the car and growling of crazies made Maddie frantic and hot as she waited for instructions. She tapped her hands on the steering wheel and looked around from window to window, checking for any cracks or weak points where the crazies could get in. Finally, the audio of a video began to play, and Vanessa turned up the volume so they could hear the instructions over the sound of the crazies.

"Place your left foot on the clutch—it'll be the pedal closest to the door—and turn the key in the ignition."

Maddie followed the instructions, and the car rumbled to life.

"With the clutch still depressed, shift into first gear." Maddie fiddled with the gear stick for a minute before it settled into first gear.

"Now, this is the tricky part. You'll want to let off the clutch very slowly at the same time as you press down on the gas with your right foot."

Maddie let off the clutch, and the car began to roll forward but only an inch or two before the crazies blocked it.

"Give it more gas," Vanessa said over the sound of the video as the crazies rocked the car with renewed vigor.

The engine revved, the car shook . . . then the engine stuttered and died.

"What happened?" Vanessa asked and paused the video.

"It stalled," Maddie replied.

"Now what?"

Maddie cranked the ignition. The engine coughed, struggling to turn over. A crazy jumped on the roof, and then another. The engine roared, and the car shook harder, the noise seeming to add to the frenzy. A crazy slammed his skull against the back window.

Vanessa cranked her neck, eyeing the rear window. "Try again. Hurry!"

Maddie scoffed. "Yeah, no pressure, just make sure you save our lives." The crazy pounded his head against the window again and a crack snaked through the glass and across the skin on his forehead.

She turned the key in the ignition again and the motor sputtered and turned over. She shifted into first and strained to hear the engine over the crazies' moans and screeches. She couldn't stall it again. Maddie clenched the steering wheel with one hand and the gearshift with the other, her knuckles white, her jaw clenched. Holding her breath, she slowly eased off the clutch and depressed the gas.

"Good, good. Keep going," Vanessa said.

Maddie sped up a bit more, pushing the crazies forward. A couple slid up the hood then fell to the side. The growls and screams of the crazies who clung to the car and dragged along sent shivers up Maddie's back. The car lurched, bouncing as if hitting speed bumps . . . a bunch, all in a row. Maddie's stomach tightened. She could almost feel the crunch of bone under the tires. The engine revved higher, and she went for the shifter again.

"Don't forget about the clutch," Vanessa said.

"Just let me drive!" Maddie pushed in the clutch and slammed the stick into second gear.

Slowly, the crazies fell away from the car as she increased her speed and cruised down the abandoned streets. Maddie looked in the side mirrors as she drove. Crazies streamed out from alleyways, likely to investigate the sound of the car. Some chased after them, but couldn't keep up.

"Great thinking on the car," Maddie said, relaxing in her seat, letting her hand off the stick and reaching forward to switch on the radio. Instead of music or obnoxious commercials, the warning to stay inside that they'd read and heard over and over again in the last week greeted them.

"Ugh, turn that off," said Vanessa, reaching for the dials.

"No, maybe there's a CD or something in here?"

The car revved and sped up a bridge and down the other side. Traffic lights continued their cycles, but no one else besides them was on the road to obey them. Maddie touched the button labelled CD and crossed her fingers some music would play. Sure enough, a song she'd just heard at the bar the other night blared over the speakers.

"Turn it down!" yelled Vanessa.

"Stop, just relax." Maddie smiled. "They can't catch us in this anyway." She switched her right hand to the wheel and touched the button on her door with her left to roll down the window, letting the air whip into the car as she danced in her seat to the beat.

Vanessa refused to even look at her, but she also didn't protest her antics.

"Come on, Nessa. We made it. Celebrate a little."

Vanessa seemed to curl into herself more and folded her arm across her sling. "We're still not safe."

"No, but when the world is ending, you have to celebrate the little things."

This time, Vanessa glanced at her friend. A smile tugged at her lips, and her shoulders began to move in time with the music.

"There you go! That's the beautiful smile I love to see."

A laugh bubbled out of Vanessa, and she danced in her seat a little more enthusiastically. Maddie began to sing and stuck her hand out the window to feel the wind move through her fingers.

She didn't know what came over her. Maybe it was the adrenaline or the energy that rushed through her over once again cheating death, but she stuck her head out the window and yelled, "We are some badass bitches!"

"Hell yeah!" Vanessa said.

"Surviving and looking fine while doing it."

"Aside from your hair."

Maddie grimaced and pulled her head back into the car. "Yeah, aside from the hair." She looked down at her hands, nail polish chipping on more than half of her nails and black dirt encrusted under the tips. "I could really use some nail polish."

Vanessa glanced over. "Yeah, me, too. Maybe if we find a safe place to stop, they'll have some."

"And some real food."

"Don't forget about some hair dye. My roots are showing."

Maddie looked at her friend. "Yeah, I can see some gray."

"Shut up! There is no gray."

Maddie snickered. "Well, no, not if you color it regularly."

"Look out!"

Maddie's eyes darted back to the road. Their car closed in on the tail end of another vehicle. Her foot found the brake and she slammed it down. Tires squealed, and Maddie closed her eyes. She heard it first. The bang and crunch of metal on metal followed by the jolt of her body being thrown against the seatbelt and then back into her chair. She couldn't move at first. Couldn't think. Her heart hammered in her chest and adrenaline coursed through her, leaving her paralyzed. Her vision swam, and she reached up to touch her forehead, then held her hand out, her fingers revealing sticky, warm blood.

"Are you okay?" Vanessa said through the ringing in her ears.

She blinked a few times, then nodded. "I think so."

"You're bleeding."

Maddie continued to stare at the blood on her fingers. "I think I hit my head." The words sounded slow and hesitant even to her muddled brain.

"We need to get out of here. That sound is gonna attract the crazies."

Crazies . . . crazies . . . Maddie unbuckled her seatbelt, opened the door, and climbed out of the car. She briefly surveyed the crumpled-in front end and then her gaze swept over to the cause of the accident. The car she'd hit just sat in the middle of the road. Empty. No passenger. No driver. No sign anyone had been in it. Just . . . abandoned.

"Well, that's safe," muttered Vanessa, opening the back door of their car and retrieving the supply pack with her good arm.

The world spun around Maddie as she stared at the car she'd hit. She reached out to steady herself on the roof of the hatchback. A few deep breaths and the world righted itself again.

"Can you walk? We need to get out of here," Vanessa said.

Maddie nodded, the motion bringing on another wave of dizziness followed by nausea. "I'm gonna have to."

They walked down the street. Maddie kept her eyes glued straight ahead, trying to combat the dizziness that threatened to send her to her knees. The nausea came in waves, but she could push through it if she just kept thinking about putting one foot in front of the other.

The more blocks they covered, the more vehicles littered the street. Some just abandoned. Some crumpled against others. Some with broken glass and blood smeared all over them. No bodies. Maddie felt a touch on her arm, and she looked over at Vanessa. She immediately regretted her decision as a more violent wave of dizziness had her knees buckling and she lowered herself to the ground, her head in her hands.

"Maddie? Maddie . . . you're not okay."

"I think . . . I think I have a concussion."

She heard a rustle of clothing and shoes scraping across concrete as Vanessa sat down beside her. "You can barely walk you're so out of it. How are we going to get over that?"

Maddie lifted her head. "Get over what?"

"That barricade."

Maddie looked to where Vanessa pointed. The vehicles were clustered closer to one another up ahead for about a block, and then her eyes settled on what appeared to be a wall of some kind. She looked at Vanessa's arm, still strapped securely in a sling. *Oh shit.* Her vision blurred and seemed to tilt. She blinked a few times and the world went upright. *We can't do this.* Maddie lowered her head into her hands again and took a deep breath. "We're going to have to climb it."

"We don't know what's on the other side."

"It can't be worse than what is on this side."

"How are we going to climb it? Between my shoulder and your head . . . "

Hopelessness saturated Vanessa's voice. It echoed what Maddie felt. But she knew she couldn't give in. She couldn't agree with her friend no matter how much she thought she was right. Someone had to keep pushing.

"Slow and steady," Maddie whispered. "We just have to push through the pain and get to the other side. We're badass bitches, remember?"

Vanessa stood and held her hand out to help Maddie up. "Then let's go."

Climbing the barricade didn't take long, but it sure hurt. Various items stacked together like a three-year-old's lego creation made up the ten-foot barricade. Garbage bins, trucks, furniture, rubble, and whatever else. It took both of them working together, but they made it over. The other side seemed quieter. There weren't as many vehicles or bodies, though blood and gore still splattered across buildings, walls, streets, and cars like a macabre painting. Maddie had thought downtown had been like something out of an apocalypse movie . . . but the east end of the city felt like a ghost-town.

They walked past department stores and a small, pathetic mall—barely more than a strip mall that couldn't possibly boast any good stores. Cars sat abandoned in parking lots, doors wide open, blood splashed on the windows. A light standard leaned on the hood of a truck, the metal crumpled underneath. A large concrete building loomed ahead to their left. No cars were in the parking lot and a big sign read COSTCO.

"There!" she said.

Vanessa looked over. "What?"

Maddie pointed to Costco. "Let's go there. It looks abandoned and it'll have all the supplies we need, plus it's super secure. Concrete walls, heavy overhead doors . . . "

"That place could be crawling with crazies."

"I can't keep going much longer, Nessa, and neither can you. I think it's our best shot."

Chapter Fifteen

Everything in One Convenient Place

Of course Vanessa wanted to go east. Ethan lived on the east side of the city. Would it be so bad just to stop by his place and see if he's okay? And if he wasn't? She didn't want to think about that. It shouldn't matter if he was okay or not. She'd called off the engagement five years ago and other than a couple of emails pleading with her to reconsider, she hadn't heard from him.

She'd lost the love of her life to principle—her independence, the importance of her career. With the world seeming to come to an end, those principles seemed shallow.

Vanessa's heart ached as she followed Maddie into the parking lot, glancing left and right, then left again, watching for crazies. Wind blew across the parking lot and ruffled her hair. Pools of blood on the worn pavement and a few abandoned cars were the only evidence something had happened here. Perhaps a battle for the fortress at one point, but a battle long over. The parking lot was silent. She shivered.

They approached the doors to the building. The exterior door was dented and bent as though someone had forced it open. A gap under the door was just big enough they'd be able to shimmy inside.

Maddie dropped to her haunches and peered underneath. She swayed and grimaced as she lifted her head. Vanessa would have to keep an eye on her if indeed she had a concussion.

Vanessa touched her shoulder. "It looks like someone broke in. Maybe this is a bad idea. What if they're still here?"

Hopefulness flashed in Maddie's eyes. "Other survivors. That would be a good thing."

"Not necessarily." She'd done enough reading on crises to know catastrophic events could bring out the worst in people. "Or there could be crazies."

"This place will have everything we need. In fact, we could just hole up here until things pass. I mean, it's Costco. They have everything."

Vanessa sighed. "Except fabulous shoes." Not that shoes mattered anymore with no one to see them, but they were her thing. That little material thing that made her feel like all was right with the world.

"True, but we could get by for a while."

It did seem like an attractive option. If there weren't any crazies running around. "Okay, we go in quietly. First hint of a problem and we leave."

"Of course."

Maddie shrugged off her backpack and lowered to her belly. She pushed her pack underneath the door, then wriggled after it. She disappeared into the warehouse store. Vanessa's heart thrummed. They'd already been chased by crazies today and narrowly escaped. Her nerves were fried. *Please let this be a safe place.*

Maddie's whisper slid under the door. "So far, so good."

Vanessa pushed her own backpack beneath the door, then lay on her stomach and wriggled inside, pain striking her shoulder as it rubbed against the concrete. Maddie waited on the other side. Hundreds of grocery carts sat on the far side of the room. Light spilled through the windows, catching on the dust they'd stirred.

They were only through the outer door. The inner door stood in front of them. It too had been damaged, one corner bent upward.

Vanessa skimmed her hand over the twisted door. Tool marks lined the metal. "This couldn't have been crazies. It looks like someone used tools to open the door. Crazies just seem to throw themselves at things until they break them open."

Maddie grinned. "That means there could be other survivors. We aren't the last ones left!" She squatted down at the opening.

Vanessa chewed on her lip for a long moment. Survivors could be a good thing. Or they could be infected with whatever this illness was. Or they could be a bunch of nut cases. Vanessa knew the dangers. There were no police to keep the law. For all intents and purposes, there was no law. They were two injured women traveling alone. Vulnerable.

Maddie poked her head inside, then turned back to look at her. "All clear." Maddie crawled inside.

Vanessa swallowed her worries and tried to grab hold of Maddie's optimism. It would be nice to see other uninfected faces. Vanessa followed.

Once inside, she climbed to her feet and adjusted her sling. Fluorescent lights beamed down from the ceiling, casting the whole store in brightness. A heavy, unpleasant sweet smell wafted on the air. Not the smell of dead bodies, but the smell of rotten fruit. Perhaps some of the fruit would still be salvageable. Her stomach growled.

Maddie took a step forward. "I'm so hungry."

Vanessa snagged her arm. "We need to search the place first. Make sure no one else is here."

Maddie sighed but agreed. They silently walked the aisles, on guard, ready to run if they saw anyone. They made their way to the back of the store. The rotting smell intensified. Fruit flies swarmed around a pallet stacked with blackened bananas. Apples glistened inside plastic bags, and Vanessa longed to grab one and sink her teeth into its tangy sweetness. No. They needed to finish their search first, and then she could gorge herself on the fruit that hadn't turned.

They crossed to the other side of the store and made their way back toward the front. With the store free of crazies and other survivors, they hurried back to the produce section. Vanessa tore open a bag of Gala apples and bit off a huge bite. The sweet juice flooded her mouth. Maddie went after the mangoes. Their "Mmms" and "Ahhs" echoed around them.

Vanessa's mouth full of apple, she said, "So good."

Maddie climbed up onto a stack of potatoes, lay down, and took another bite of plum. "We should stay here forever."

Vanessa sprawled beside her. "We should. Costco is our new home." She laughed. It sounded weird to her own ears. It's a sound she hadn't heard much of since this whole ordeal began. Vanessa's eyes grew heavy. It was only early evening, but the week's turmoil had taken its toll. She sat up. "I'm going to find some sheets and blankets and a mattress."

"Good plan. And pillows."

"You're right. This is the perfect place to be. It has everything we need." Maybe they'd be okay waiting out the epidemic here.

They located pillows, some 800-thread-count Egyptian cotton sheets, and a bed-in-a-bag set. They pulled a mattress off the metal shelving and dragged it around to the seasonal section. They tore open a tent box, erected the massive structure to keep the fluorescents from burning into their eyes while they tried to sleep, and then tugged the mattress inside.

They dressed the bed in the linens, then crawled inside. For a moment, Vanessa was transported back to her childhood when she and Maddie would camp out in their backyards. "Just like when we were kids."

Maddie giggled and rolled onto her belly. "Ghost stories?"

Vanessa smiled. "You go first."

They told each other stories that were more funny than scary. They were living a real horror. They didn't need any more of it.

Vanessa closed her eyes and drifted off.

A voice. Low and loud. Shouting.

Vanessa's eyes fluttered open. Legs filled the tent door. A guy with a week's worth of scruff and a rifle at his shoulder peered in at them. "Who the hell are you?"

Chapter Sixteen

Zombies. Undead. Rotting, Brain-Eating Freaks

Maddie felt someone jostle her shoulder. Refusing to open her eyes, she whined, "Whaaaat?"

"Maddie, wake up."

"Go away," she moaned, blindly swatting at Vanessa.

"Hey!" barked an unfamiliar, masculine voice.

There's not supposed to be anyone here.

"I asked you a question. Who the hell are you?"

Maddie bolted up and immediately regretted her swift movement as the world spun for a moment before the haze passed. *Right, concussion, take it slow.* She stared at a rough-looking face that matched the voice. Facial hair covered most of his features, but his hard eyes held no forgiveness and no leeway. He wanted the answer he wanted and anything other than that didn't seem as if it would bode well for her and Vanessa.

Vanessa pulled the comforter to her chest. "We're just some survivors. We got run out of downtown and needed a place to stay."

The guy grunted. "Downtown? No one's come out of the city center in at least three days. No way you two survived. No way."

The barricade must have stopped people . . . "Well, we did." Maddie lifted her chin. "Why are we any less capable than anyone else of surviving?"

The man lifted an eyebrow and looked at her, his expression saying, "Are you kidding me?" His hand went to a huge machete-type knife strapped to his hip. His other hand held a gun. Maddie didn't know exactly what kind of gun, but it didn't really matter. A gun was a gun was a gun in her mind. They all shot bullets, and she couldn't outrun bullets. Crazies, sure. Bullets, not so much.

"We holed up in our apartment for a week," Maddie said. "We had enough supplies to last us that long."

The guy nodded, his brows furrowing. "Okay. That I can believe. But how did you get past the zombies and the wall?"

Maddie felt her eyes widen, and she looked over at Vanessa. She'd paled, and she licked her lips.

"Zombies?" Vanessa squeaked out.

"Yeah. Zombies. Undead. Rotting, brain-eating freaks. Zombies. What the hell did you think they were?"

"We've just been calling them crazies. Undead?" Maddie couldn't quite believe it . . . and yet it made sense.

"See! I told you that guy in the drug store was walking!" Vanessa said.

Maddie frowned. "What?"

"The guy I killed with the bat. You basically said I was crazy, and that he'd been dead a while. Well, zombies *walk.*"

"We were both right."

"Enough!" barked out Burly-man. "Get out of the tent and come with me. The others are going to be here soon, and we need to check you over."

Vanessa hesitated in the doorway of the tent. "Check us over?"

"There is *no way* any guys are checking us over." Maddie climbed out behind Vanessa and stood tall, staring Burly-man in the eye. *Shit, he's tall. And large. And muscular. Too bad his face isn't anything to look at . . . okay, that's off topic . . .*

"If there's any chance you're going to stay here with us—and I'm not saying there is—we need to be sure you're clean. Only way to do that is to check you over for injuries."

Maddie looked over at Vanessa, and their eyes met. Vanessa shook her head, and Maddie nodded her agreement. They'd rather take their chances with the crazies—no, *zombies*, apparently—than with a group of men.

"I think we'll just leave," said Vanessa.

Burly-man smiled, but it left Maddie feeling cold and scared. "Sorry, no can do."

"What? Why not?" Maddie asked, her brow furrowing in confusion.

"Can't have you going out and telling other survivors about where we are and what we got. We cleared this place out. We secured it. And we're keeping it secured. Word gets out that Costco is a safe house and this place will be overrun. Nope, sorry, ladies, but you're stuck with us until we decide what to do with you."

Maddie shook her head. "No. You can't keep us here."

Burly-man chuckled and pulled his knife out of its sheath. Her gaze ran over the blade from the hilt down the gleaming metal all the way to the needle-sharp tip. She shuddered. "Oh, really? I can't?" He turned the blade back and forth. The fluorescent lights glinted off the metal.

Maddie opened her mouth to say something, but Vanessa touched her arm and shook her head. *Right, keep my mouth shut before I get us into any more trouble.*

Vanessa offered an uneasy smile. "Look, I'm sure we can come to some kind of agreement."

Burly-man shrugged and put the knife away. "Let's go sit down and wait for the others." He tilted his head, indicating he wanted them to walk in front of him.

Maddie took Vanessa's hand in hers and squeezed it. No way she'd let anything happen to them. No way. And if she could outrun zombies, she could outrun Burly-man. *As long as he doesn't go for his gun.* But loud noises attracted crazies, so she was counting on the gun being his last resort.

They walked toward the food court at the front of the store. The big overhead door loomed ahead of them, mostly closed, but still open just enough they could roll under. Vanessa's hand tightened on hers. That was all the confirmation Maddie needed. She sprang forward in a sprint, tugging Vanessa along. Burly-man's shouts and pounding footsteps thundered and echoed through the warehouse. Maddie's heart rate sped.

At the door, she stopped and released Vanessa's hand. "Go!"

Vanessa dropped to the floor and rolled under the door, disappearing on the other side. Maddie followed. Springing to her feet, ready to sprint to the next door, she searched for Vanessa.

Vanessa stood, right beside her, staring at a group of five men just inside the second door. "Ethan?"

Chapter Seventeen

Old News is New Again

Vanessa's arms went limp. She was supposed to be running away. She was supposed to be trying to escape. She was supposed to be breathing, but that wasn't happening either.

Ethan stood before her, a little older and a little hairier than the last time she saw him, but still just as stunning. His eyes narrowed. "Vanessa?"

She opened her mouth to speak, but what could she say after all this time? She wanted to tell him she was stupid to break up, and how she'd missed him over the last five years, but instead she said, "You have a beard." *Smooth, Vanessa. Really smooth.*

The other four guys eyed Ethan, then Vanessa. His Adam's apple bobbed up and down. "You survived?" His gaze darted to her feet, clad in her wedge heels. "You?"

Maddie hitched her hand on her hip. "What the hell is that supposed to mean?"

He scratched the back of his head. "Just, uh, thought someone like you—"

Vanessa bristled. "Someone like me?"

Burly-guy slid under the door and jumped to his feet. He grabbed Vanessa's arm, crushing her biceps and wrenching her sore shoulder. She drew a hissed breath.

Ethan reached for her. "Hey, Chad, that's enough. I know her."

Chad smirked. "You know her, huh?" His gaze slid over her, a sensation as disgusting as that goo from the popper.

Ethan stepped forward. "Yeah, I know her, which means you're not going to."

Chad released Vanessa's arm. "You can tell her and her friend, then, that they can't leave, and we need to check them over."

Ethan shifted from one foot to the other. "I'll take care of it."

Chad's slimy gaze flashed to Maddie.

Ethan rested his hand on the gun in the holster at his hip. "And the other one too."

"You're not touching me, asshole," Maddie said.

Ethan shifted again. "We have to check. We can't let someone bring the disease in here. You have to understand that."

Maddie folded her arms. "Fuck that."

Vanessa nudged Maddie. "Let's just go along then we can stay here. You said you wanted to stay here forever."

"Not with them." Maddie waved her hands over them.

Vanessa found Ethan's green eyes. "We'll be safe. It'll be good."

Maddie looked from Vanessa to Ethan. "What the hell is wrong with you? He's old news."

Vanessa looked down at her feet.

Maddie glowered at her. "He's old news, right?"

Moisture stinging her eyes, Vanessa looked away from Maddie's accusing gaze. She thought she'd never see him again. There was this sliver of hope she'd clung to, and now he was here in front of her. Checking her over for wounds didn't sound so bad.

Maddie sighed and shook her head. It's the one thing she'd kept from Maddie. Was it pride? Or just a special secret she wanted to protect? She didn't know.

"Follow me." Ethan motioned to them.

He led them toward the tire department. Maddie slipped her arm around Vanessa's and whispered in her ear, "We can't stay here with these guys."

Vanessa sunk her teeth into her bottom lip. "It might be safer with them."

"Did you see the way Chad looked at us? He was practically salivating. A bunch of guys? No girls? What do you think they're after?"

Vanessa's jaw tightened.

Ethan pushed the glass door open and waved them in. Vanessa and Maddie stepped inside, and Ethan closed the door behind them. "Look," he said. "I know this is going to be awkward, but I kind need to see—everything."

Maddie flushed. "This is a violation."

Ethan sighed. "I know, but who are you going to report it to? The police? They don't exist anymore. There's another group of survivors occupying Walmart. You'll be in far worse shape if they find you."

"I'll go first." Vanessa stepped forward. "Then you'll see it's going to be okay." The back of her neck warmed. She shouldn't have been so happy to take off her clothes for Ethan. It's the fricking Zombie Apocalypse, and she was mooning over her ex. Logically, she knew it was ridiculous, but that didn't stop her heart from racing.

Vanessa peeled off her shoes first and placed her bare feet on the cool concrete. Then, she removed the sling, unfastened her top button, and pulled her shirt off over her head. She'd worn her leopard print bra, thank goodness.

Next, she peeled off her pants. Damn it, she hadn't worn the matching panties. She'd gone for comfort with some cotton briefs. Oh, well. Maybe he'd be too enamored with the bra to notice her underwear.

"The underwear too." He shrugged. "Sorry." He looked down at the floor and kicked an imaginary stone.

Vanessa slid out of her underwear, unhooked her bra and dropped it on the floor. Thank goodness for yoga. She knew she was in better shape than when he saw her last.

"Okay, um. I'm just going to look you over." He walked around the back of her. He gently pushed her hair off her neck. She shivered. "All good back here," he said.

He walked around to the front. He swallowed hard as he looked from head to toe and back to head. He peered into her eyes. "All good here too." She got lost there for a long moment as he held her gaze. She'd missed him so much.

Maddie cleared her throat. "Do you want me to leave you two alone?"

Vanessa blinked to break the spell. "Uh, no. I'm just— I—"

Ethan took a deep breath. "No, uh, we're done. Your turn."

"Great." Maddie rolled her eyes.

She roughly shoved off her clothes and dropped them on the floor. She spread her arms. "Go ahead. Take a look."

Ethan finished his inspection, they dressed, then he led Vanessa and Maddie back into the warehouse. Vanessa couldn't take her eyes off Ethan. He was here. With her. Well, not with her-with her, but close to her.

Ethan turned to her. "Would you want to . . . talk?" He looked as unsure as a fifteen-year-old boy asking a girl to a dance.

"Maddie, I'll meet you back at the tent."

Maddie smirked. "Oh, okay. Have a good talk." She framed the word "talk" with quote fingers then walked off.

Vanessa's cheeks warmed, and she rubbed her bad arm. She wanted to look at him, but she didn't. She felt like she was wearing five years of longing on her face. She felt pathetic and, at the same time, exhilarated to be with him again.

He looked up at the ceiling then back to her. "It's good to see you again."

Her pulse raced. "You too." *Words. Come on, Vanessa, pull it together.* Deep breath. "I didn't think . . . with all of this . . . I'd ever . . . ."

"You had to know I'd survive. I survived something much worse five years ago." He blinked and looked down.

An ache broke out in her chest. She knew she hurt him but to see the pain on his face this many years later? Excruciating. "I'm so sorry. I-I felt like . . . ."

"Look, I don't want to dredge up the past. I just wanted to tell you . . . ." He looked down, and his cheeks flushed.

A loud metallic bang echoed around the store. Ethan's head shot up. Another bang—different this time—as though a hundred separate noises joined to create one deafening sound.

"They're here!" Ethan's shout tore through the store.

Chapter Eighteen

Is Anywhere Really Safe Anymore?

Maddie walked toward the tent, leaving Vanessa behind with Ethan. Of all the people to run into, Ethan was the last thing Vanessa needed. She was vulnerable right now. Hell, Maddie felt vulnerable and none of her exes were here. She'd seen the way Vanessa looked at him, the way she blushed like a little school girl when Ethan had been looking her over. Vanessa felt something, and that was bad news.

She grabbed a pair of athletic shoes on her way back to the tent and slipped them on. Rather than climb into the tent, she paced back and forth in front of it. She knew she should respect Vanessa's request to be alone, but it took everything in her to keep from interfering. *Nessa is an adult. She can make her own decisions and her own mistakes.*

But she didn't want to see her friend make any mistakes. She didn't want to see her hurt . . . but the look on Nessa's face made it abundantly clear to her that no matter what happened, what was said or done, she wasn't coming out of this run-in unscathed.

A bang echoed through the store, and Maddie stopped dead in her tracks. She looked around for the source of the noise.

"They're here!" bellowed Ethan's warning cry.

That was all Maddie needed to hear. She grabbed the two backpacks out of the tent, slung one over each shoulder, and sprinted toward the tire center where she'd left Vanessa.

The group of six men all gathered by the shopping carts, pulling out a coterie of weapons and stacking tires and carts as barricades in front of the door.

She looked around for Vanessa and saw her with Ethan just outside the tire center doorway. Vanessa held his hand.

She's just scared. It's a comfort thing, nothing more, Maddie told herself, walking over to her friend.

"Who's 'they'? The crazies, I mean, zombies?" asked Maddie.

Ethan nodded. "We ran into a horde when we were out. We thought we lost them, but I guess they followed us."

"But we can fight them off, right? This place is safe."

Ethan shrugged. "Is anywhere really safe anymore?"

Maddie couldn't bring herself to respond to that, and by Vanessa's silence, the truth wasn't a welcome one to her either. There had to be somewhere safe. *Somewhere.* Maybe it wasn't here, but if they got out, if they got far enough away . . .

How far could it have spread?

Another loud bang and the overhead door shook. A snarling, decaying face appeared under the door. Chad lunged with his machete and plunged it into the zombie's neck, slicing off its head with a sickening crunch. Maddie's stomach churned; her eyes focused on the pool of reddish-black fluid that seeped out of the neck stump. Another head appeared and another guy took it out. They swung knives, axes, and a sledgehammer, leaving the guns alone. *Probably preserving bullets.* For now.

Another crazy made it through. One of the men plunged an ax into the crazy's head and then yanked the bloody weapon back out as the crazy fell to its knees. He then swung it at the neck of another, only severing part of its head, a spirt of blood coming out of an artery like a fountain as the crazy continued its attack and the man swung the ax yet again to finish the job.

Maddie stared, unable to look away. Two crazies ran toward Chad, one after the other. Chad lifted his machete and swung it down, burying it in the skulls of both crazies.

Ethan tugged at Vanessa's hand. "Come with me."

Maddie looked up at him. She didn't want to trust him. She didn't even want to be near him. *He's not a bad guy.* He'd never been a bad guy, and right now, he was their best chance.

Vanessa resisted a bit, pulling against Ethan. "Where are we going?"

Ethan didn't allow Vanessa to slow him down. He strode toward the inner door, towing Vanessa behind. "I'm getting you away from here."

After a moment of hesitation, another severed zombie head rolled across the floor, and Maddie hurried after them.

He led them toward the back of the store, past towering shelves and then through pallets wrapped in plastic. The lights weren't as garish and bright. They created shadows in every corner. Maddie glanced around, her eyes darting to every potential hiding place. Anyone or anything could be hiding back here.

Ethan led them to another overhead door at the back of the store. Back here, it was quiet. No zombies moaning or groaning or banging on metal, which hopefully meant it was clear on the other side. Ethan pressed a green button on the wall and the door let out a loud whirr as it went up slightly, just enough for someone to roll under.

Ethan dropped Vanessa's hand and turned it, palm up, and placed keys in her hand, then closed her fingers around them. "There's a truck just outside. It's full of supplies. Get in and drive east out of the city. Don't come back."

Maddie watched her friend's face. Vanessa looked torn. Pain widened her eyes, and her lips turned down. "What about you?"

"I gotta go help the others."

Vanessa tried to take his hand again, but he pulled it away. "They're not going to take it too well you sent us away with the emergency escape plan."

"I'll be fine."

Maddie sighed. More than anything, she wanted to get Vanessa away from Ethan, but she couldn't leave him here. *If they managed to fight off the zombies and not get overrun, there was no way his buddies would forgive him for ruining their contingency plan.*

"She's right." Maddie hated that she said the words but knew she had to. "You need to come with us. If the zombies don't kill you, the guys will."

Ethan shook his head. "They're my friends. I'll be fine."

"They're in!" came a shout from the far side of the store—barely audible from here—followed by a series of gunshots. With each echoing bang, Maddie jumped a little.

Ethan looked at Vanessa. "You have to go now. Go!" He reached behind his back and pulled a large pistol out of his waistband and handed it to Maddie. Their eyes met, no words said, and she nodded. She'd look after Vanessa.

Vanessa shook her head. "Not without you."

A slight smile tugged at Ethan's lips. "You left me before, you can do it again. Go."

Maddie nodded at him. More gunshots thundered and shouts made it hard to tell if the men were winning or losing the fight, but she knew she and Vanessa were running out of time. She tossed her backpack and then Vanessa's out the door and crouched down.

"Come on, Nessa, let's go."

She shook her head and reached for Ethan's hand. "Please, come with us."

"I can't abandon them," he said.

Maddie's heart ached for Vanessa, the pain in her voice, the hurt in Ethan's eyes. This was the last thing they needed.

"I can't leave you to die," Vanessa said. "I can't live with that."

Voices and gunshots grew louder and Maddie knew that the zombies had breached the first door, at the very least. It wouldn't be long before they overran the store.

"Nessa, let's go. Now!" She reached for her hand. She looked at Ethan and silently pled with him to help.

Gunshots grew faster and more frenzied; a scream of pain carried through the store. Ethan's face changed from hurt to determination and his jaw set. He crouched down by the door and tugged at Vanessa's hand. "Out, let's go."

"You're coming with?" Vanessa asked.

"You're giving me very little choice." Another scream, guttural and angry. "I like my life." He gave her a nudge.

Maddie rolled under the door and stood, then picked up the backpacks and tossed them into the bed of the waiting king cab truck. Vanessa and Ethan slid under the door and hurried for the truck. Maddie threw open the passenger door and climbed into the backseat. Vanessa climbed in on the driver's side and slid across the bench to the passenger seat and pulled the door closed. Ethan stood beside the overhead door, not moving, just looking and listening.

"Come on!" shouted Maddie. The sounds of death and pain and the stench of crazies wafted under the door and into the truck. The undead were close. Too close.

Ethan hesitated a moment longer and a bloody hand lashed out under the door followed by Chad's face. Red speckled his face, and he reached for Ethan. "Help me!"

Ethan stared. Frozen.

Maddie leaned over the seat. "Ethan! It's too late! Come on!" But he didn't move. *He's not going to come.* She climbed over the seat. She'd have to drive them out of here. She slammed the heavy pistol on the dash and held out her hand to Vanessa. "Keys!"

Vanessa fisted her hand around them. "We're not leaving without him."

"Nessa, don't do this. Keys!"

A ragged breath and she tossed the keys at Maddie.

She turned the key and the truck rumbled to life.

"Ethan!" called Vanessa.

He didn't move.

"ETHAN!"

Maddie put the truck in drive. "We have to go."

"No, just a few more seconds." Quiet. Simple. Firm. Vanessa's resolve scared her. Hysteria and fear—those were emotions that fit here. A quiet calm, like the lack of wind just before a storm hit, sent terror through Maddie.

"Don't, Nessa. Don't."

Vanessa looked away and, before Maddie could stop her, she jumped out of the truck and sprinted toward Ethan. She tugged at his hand, but he didn't look away from Chad, who continued to scream at him—this time just noises, not words. Maddie couldn't even imagine what was happening to him on the other side of that overhead door.

"Ethan, you need to come with me," Maddie heard Vanessa shout. "It's too late for your friends, but it's not too late for you. I never should have left you the way I did, and I'm not going to leave you behind now."

Maddie swallowed the lump in her throat. *Ethan, if you're the death of her, I swear . . .*

Ethan looked from Chad to Vanessa. His free hand went to her face. *What are they doing? We have to go!* But it was like there was a bubble around her and Ethan and they were in their own world.

His lips touched hers for just a minute, then his whole body came alive, and he lunged toward the truck, dragging Vanessa with him.

"In," he commanded, once again taking charge.

Vanessa climbed up and into the backseat.

Ethan leaped into the passenger seat and slammed the door. Maddie threw the truck into drive and slammed her foot on the gas. The engine protested and tires squealed, then got traction and tore off. Once out of the parking lot, Maddie looked over at the store. Zombies converged on the front door, the metal bent in and mangled.

How do we keep cheating death? She slowed the truck to a more manageable speed and set her eyes on the road ahead, weaving around parked and abandoned vehicles.

Chapter Nineteen

Where Did all the Bodies Go?

The last rays of the day's orange sunlight lightened Ethan's hair as he leaned his head against the window and stared out at the passing scenery. "I shouldn't have left them."

Vanessa reached over the seat and took his hand, threading her fingers between his. "You just would have died too."

He pressed his eyes closed then open again. "Is that such a bad thing?"

"It is to me," Vanessa said.

Maddie floored it through a red light. She let out an exasperated sigh. "What's done is done. We need to focus." She swerved around an abandoned car.

Vanessa leaned into Ethan. Every touch was a pleasant sensation on her skin. She wanted to be closer. Maddie glanced over at her and shook her head in tight movements. Vanessa looked away from her disapproving stare.

Up ahead, the bridge that carried them over the floodway and out of the city stretched its concrete supports.

Maddie's grip tightened on the steering wheel. "Shit."

Vanessa followed her gaze through the windshield. "Shit" wasn't a strong enough word. Abandoned cars filled the road, every lane packed tight. The unrelenting traffic jam stretched a quarter of a mile, all the way over the bridge. Probably from people trying to escape the city. Doors stood open. And blood. So much blood. A lead weight settled into Vanessa's stomach.

Ethan pushed his fingers through his hair. "We're going to have to go on foot from here."

Maddie slowed the truck and stopped. She put it in park and turned off the engine. All three silently sat staring out the window at the empty cars and the gore. Vanessa didn't want to leave the safety of the truck cab.

"We stay together. Don't close the doors when we get out. No talking. No noise at all." He looked down at Vanessa's feet. "Lose the shoes."

"What? No. I can run in them."

"The sound when they hit the pavement."

"I can't go barefoot." She eyed the smashed windshields and the bits of glass littering the pavement. "There's broken glass."

Ethan sighed and carefully pulled the door handle. She'd won. She got to keep her shoes a little longer. Logically, her attachment to her footwear didn't make sense, but somehow losing them seemed like losing a little piece of herself. The world was ending, but she still wanted to be Vanessa. Her shoes were the last thing that truly made sense.

Ethan climbed out of the truck, and Vanessa followed. Maddie grabbed the pistol from the dash and rounded the front of the vehicle to join them. They all shrugged into their backpacks. Ethan put his finger to his lips. Silence. He walked forward, and Vanessa tiptoed after him.

Wind whipped Vanessa's hair, and a drizzle of rain raised goosebumps on her arms as they walked toward the bridge. In the distance, lightning tore jagged lines in the sky and thunder rumbled against the eerie silence. She pressed her eyes closed for a moment and imagined the chaos as people tried to leave the city—men, women, children—and then something went terribly wrong. Still, there were no bodies. Where were they?

She stepped onto the bridge and over glass to keep it from crunching underfoot. She glanced into a mini-van window. A car seat. Blood stained the restraint straps. A small shoe lay on the ground. Her chest tightened. *Oh, my . . . .*

It was as if the full weight of everything that had happened settled onto her shoulders at that moment. An enormous tidal wave of fear rolled over her. She froze. Ethan motioned her forward. Tears formed on her lower lashes, blurring her vision. Maddie looked down at the baby shoe, then to Vanessa. She whispered, "Let's just keep going, Nessa."

Vanessa pulled in a breath and forced her feet forward. Wind whooshed under the bridge. They made it to the center. Halfway. They were almost there. She didn't like this—feeling trapped on the bridge with only one direction they could go. Another bottleneck. A tapping sound rattled under the bridge. She leaned sideways to see what was making the sound. As she did, a gust of wind carried that heavy, putrid smell that had become so familiar.

Death.

Within the shadow cast by the bridge, crazies, hundreds of them, huddled around dozens of bodies, took bites and pulled off chunks of flesh. That tapping sound—their teeth gnashing. Her breath caught. A single sound and they'd be pouring onto the bridge. She backed away from the edge.

Ethan mouthed, "What?"

She pointed down and mouthed, "Crazies."

Maddie's eyes widened. Ethan stepped closer to the guardrail and glanced downward, then leaned away. All the color drained from his cheeks.

He picked up his pace, silently hurrying toward the end of the bridge and the end of the traffic jam. Maddie kept up with him. Vanessa couldn't move that fast on her toes, and the heels of her shoes would surely draw their attention. She hurried forward, but lost her balance and stepped sideways. A piece of glass crunched underfoot.

Moans carried from under the bridge. A gray-faced crazy appeared behind them at the other end of the structure. A dozen more joined him.

"Run!" Maddie cried.

They took off, full stride toward the end of the bridge. Crazies poured after them like a river of violent flesh. Her feet pounded against the pavement. Howls and screeches grew louder with each step.

Ethan and Maddie ran several paces ahead of her. She glanced back. A crazy sprinted up behind her, his arms extended, only inches from her hair. Ethan looked back and drew his gun. He stopped and dashed back to her. He lifted the gun. Vanessa kept running. She sprinted past him. An explosion deafened her. She glanced over her shoulder. The crazy, a crater in his forehead and gray matter sliding over his nose, stumbled sideways and fell to the ground, but ten more sprinted toward her to take his place. Ethan grabbed her hand and towed her forward. She pushed her legs faster.

Maddie jumped into a sedan at the end of the bridge. Vanessa and Ethan scrambled inside and slammed and locked the doors. Crazies hit the car, throwing themselves against the glass. The rear window cracked. Maddie cranked the key, still in the ignition. The engine coughed, but refused to start. She cranked again. Still nothing.

Vanessa gripped the leather seat. "Come on, Maddie!"

"I'm trying!"

"Pump the gas," Ethan shouted.

Maddie pushed her foot against the gas pedal. The roof dented as crazies jumped onto the car. Maddie cranked again. The engine fired, and she threw it in drive. The car lurched forward, but dozens of crazies blocked their path. She floored it and the engine roared. A crazy dropped in front of her. The car bounced as she ran over the body. Vanessa peered out the window and dark liquid sprayed onto the pavement.

Ethan waved his hand. "Go! Go! Go!"

"I've got it floored. There are too many of them."

Chapter Twenty

Only the Beginning

Maddie kept the gas floored, slowly pushing through the throngs of zombies… crazies… whatever they were. *We will survive. We will survive,* she repeated over and over in her head. She just had to get past these zombies, and they'd be okay. They'd be out of the city and away from populated areas. They'd be fine. They had to be. *Mom said that outside of the city it was quiet.*

The car struggled with every meter it gained. The horde pushed against it, hundreds of zombies trying to get at them. A crack sounded and Vanessa screamed. Maddie glanced over to see the window beside Vanessa had web-like fissures and blood smeared across it. Another blow or two and they'd get through. Time counted down and with it so did their chances of survival.

"Keep going!" screamed Vanessa as lightning streaked across the sky again and the sounds of zombies beating on the car mixed with the sound of pelting rain.

Thunder cracked and the zombies stopped. The car lurched forward, bouncing over a few bodies that fell under the tires. They kept going, picking up speed. Thunder rumbled and all around the vehicle the heads of zombies turned up.

"The thunder . . ." she breathed out, scared to make any noise that might renew the zombies' interest in them.

"It's confusing them," finished Ethan. "Keep going."

They came to a stoplight. She slowed down. More cars littered the highway ahead. Ethan pointed left. "Let's take the backroads. Turn here."

She turned left onto a different highway, this one almost devoid of all vehicles or signs of life—or undead. At the first road, she turned right onto a gravel road and headed east again. The windshield wipers whipped back and forth, but couldn't keep up with the downpour. The rain and the growing darkness swallowed the road ahead.

"We need to find a place to wait out the night," Vanessa said.

In the flashing lightning, grasses bent by the storm lined one side of the road, shadowed trees guarded the other. "It looks pretty abandoned out here. Maybe there'll be a house where we can stop to sleep before we keep going."

Ethan nodded and pointed ahead as they crested a rise in the road. "There. Looks like a driveway cutting into those trees. Let's see if there's a house."

Maddie looked where he pointed and nodded. Lightning split the sky, illuminating the roof that peeked through the trees. The three of them remained silent as she turned the car onto the driveway. The house was massive. A wraparound deck, three-car garage, two stories, the yard immaculate in the blue-green flashes of lightning. It looked untouched by the horrors of the past week. Everywhere they'd gone there had been evidence of change, but here no blood, no abandoned vehicles, no stench of death.

Safe haven, thought Maddie, but she pushed the thought out of her mind. *Don't jinx it. Nowhere is safe. This is just a rest stop.*

"Pull up by the garage," Ethan said and Maddie complied, though a part of her chaffed he had taken charge. She and Vanessa had been doing just fine on their own, and they didn't need him to tell them what to do. After all, he'd be dead if not for Nessa risking her life for him.

Putting the car in park, she looked at Ethan and reluctantly said, "What's the plan?"

"Keep the car running. I'll go in and make sure the coast is clear."

She nodded. "Fine."

"You can't go in alone," said Vanessa.

Ethan smiled. "I'm not putting you in a dangerous situation, and I'm not okay with leaving you here alone, so the only option is for you girls to stay here while I check things out."

"You girls"? Maddie ground her teeth. She peered over the backseat at Vanessa, restraining an eye roll. "It's fine, Vanessa. He'll be fine." *Better him than us.* She cringed at the thought. She shouldn't be like that. Survivors needed to stick together, needed to look out for each other, and thinking ill toward Ethan wasn't fair. If not for him, they probably wouldn't have made it out of Costco.

With no other further protest, he opened the door, got out, and slammed it shut. He paused and Maddie held her breath, waiting to see if the noise brought anyone—or anything—out to investigate. Water continued to pummel the car but besides the noises from the storm, there were no other sounds. Maybe it would be okay here? Maybe. But did she dare hope?

The car remained silent. Neither her nor Vanessa said a word. They waited, bated breath, for Ethan to return with the all clear.

Please, thought Maddie. *We need this. We need a break.*

How much time had passed? The house was huge, and it would take some time to check every room.

"Shouldn't he be back by now?" Vanessa squirmed in her seat.

"No. Give him some more time." *Be calm for Nessa.* "I didn't realize you missed him so much. You never mentioned him after you broke off the engagement."

Vanessa looked at her and offered a sad smile. "I didn't really either. I don't know, maybe it's fate . . . ." She pulled something out of her pocket and held it out to Maddie. She took it and looked it over.

Maddie turned the photo of Ethan and a happy, younger Vanessa over in her hand. "You kept this?"

"I'd forgotten all about it until I went for the cash. It was there. I couldn't leave it behind. And then he showed up in the middle of the Apocalypse—"

"Don't use that word." Maddie's insides clenched at the thought this could be it. The end. She'd used the word plenty in the past week. Back before she really believed it could be true.

"Whatever you want to call it, it's almost like the world is giving me one last chance to get my priorities straight."

Priorities straight? "What do you mean by that? We had a pretty good life."

Vanessa nodded. "I just mean that I feel like I'm getting a chance to use what little time we have left to make things right with Ethan."

Maddie stared at the windshield, pelted by rain, the sky flashing with almost constant lightning. "Don't talk like that. We've made it this far. We're gonna survive this thing."

"I doubt it."

"So, what? You're just going to accept that and wait for the end? Where's your fight? Your hope?"

"No, I'm going to make the most of the time I have left."

Maddie shook her head and looked at her, waiting for their eyes to meet before she spoke. "Work up a little fight. You're being ridiculous, and with an attitude like that you probably won't make it."

"Don't be naive, Maddie. You keep putting your head in the sand about everything. Life is never serious for you. Well, guess what, I'm being the realist here."

"No, you're so scared of daring to hope that you quit while you're ahead. That's why you broke things off with Ethan. You just hide behind your job."

"You're one to talk. You never get serious with any guy. And as for jobs, you're a secretary. At least I've been engaged *and* I had a career. "

Maddie stared at the water streaming down the windshield. "I'm an assistant."

"*Was*. And it's the same thing."

Maddie clutched the steering wheel tighter and took a deep breath. "The difference is, I take risks to get ahead. I'm not afraid to gamble a little. You don't. Even now, you are only considering fixing things with Ethan because you're convinced you're going to die soon anyway. What do you have to lose? 'Til death do us part is a lot closer now than it was before."

"That's not true." Maddie glanced over to see Vanessa reach up and trace the crack in the window with her fingertips.

"No? You mean to tell me you'd be this into Ethan if you didn't think it was the end of the world?"

"Yes."

Maddie shook her head. "Hard truth time, Vanessa—you wouldn't. You could have reached out to him at any time in the last few years and you didn't. But Ethan aside, you need to stop being scared and decide to fight 'cause I'm not gonna leave you behind, and I sure as hell ain't planning on dying."

Maddie waited for her reaction, any reaction—anger, sadness, relief—some kind of emotion that told Maddie she'd gotten through to her and that she wanted to live. They'd fought so hard, they'd made it this far. She couldn't give up now. Not when they might finally have a chance to recuperate.

Vanessa let out a sigh, and Maddie expected her to voice her concession but instead she pointed. "He's back."

Maddie looked out to see Ethan standing by the west side of the garage. She had to squint to see him through the storm. "What's he holding?" she asked as the lightning reflected off of something he held high and shook back and forth in a triumphant sort of gesture.

"I think that's wine." Vanessa's voice hinted at awe.

"Really?"

"What else would that bottle be?"

Maddie shrugged and reached into the backseat for her backpack. "True. It better not be some of that homemade stuff. My dad makes some out of his blueberries and it's so gross."

She opened the car door and cold air and rain blasted at her. She shivered, hunkered down, and sprinted toward Ethan. Vanessa joined her. The three of them ran together along the garage to a side door. Ethan slammed the door shut behind them, deadening the noise from the storm.

Ethan flicked a switch and illuminated the garage with harsh florescent light. "Wait until you see the place."

Maddie glanced around the huge, three-car garage. There were no vehicles in it, but tools lay scattered around a workbench and canned goods were stacked along a far wall as well as a huge deep freeze near the door to the house.

"But first, this is for you." Ethan handed Maddie a bottle of wine.

Maybe he isn't so bad after all. Maddie turned the bottle over to read the label. Bin 555. This was good stuff. Whoever owned this house had, at the very least, decent taste in wine, which made her hopeful.

Ethan climbed a couple of wooden steps and opened the door into the house. A soft glowing light lit up the back entrance, and they walked in. He led them down a tiled hall around a staircase and into a kitchen that was probably the size of Maddie's entire apartment. She looked around in appreciation and then pulled out a barstool and sat down at the island. Vanessa didn't sit with her, though.

Ethan turned to a glass cupboard and pulled out a few stemless wine glasses and placed them on the granite island, then turned back and grabbed a fancy-looking corkscrew from the same cabinet.

Maddie slid her bottle over to him, and he got to work removing the cork. The pop followed by the glug of pouring wine was music to her ears.

He passed out the glasses, keeping one for himself, and raised his glass. "To us, for making it this far."

"To us," Maddie said, clinking Ethan's glass.

Vanessa didn't mimic the sentiment, though. Instead, she stared at her wine and remained silent.

"Want to explore the place a little?" he asked.

Vanessa looked up at him and the excitement in her eyes didn't go unnoticed. "Yes."

As much as Maddie also wanted to look around, she knew Vanessa well enough to know she wanted some alone time with Ethan. "I think I'll just stay here. I'm so tired all I want to do is sit, relax, drink wine, and pretend the outside world hasn't gone to shit."

Ethan chuckled. "I don't blame you. All right, Nessa, let me give you the grand tour of your castle."

Hearing someone else call her "Nessa" hit Maddie and left her reeling. For as long as she could remember, she'd been the only one close enough to Vanessa to call her that.

The two walked off, wine glasses in hand, toward the staircase and soon disappeared upstairs. Maddie got down from the barstool and carried her glass of wine to the living room, settled down on the couch, and threw her feet up. She stared at them, all dirty and gross and in desperate need of a pedicure—the only sign something was wrong in this otherwise-untouched house.

Maddie took a sip of her wine and savored the sweet and bitter flavor before swallowing it, then leaned back and closed her eyes. Rain drummed outside and thunder rolled and the sound of Vanessa laughing drifted down the stairs. Right here, right now, everything was okay. There was no Apocalypse. There was no death, decay, horror, or violence. No Vanessa mad at her. No fighting or running. Just her and this glass of wine for however long it lasted.

But, something inside her told her this wasn't the end of their suffering.

It was only the beginning.

Acknowledgements

It's been a very neat experience to co-author a book, but because you just can't take this book too seriously, it's also been a good reminder of what it's like to write purely for the love of a story and not just to further our careers. It's so easy to get lost in the book industry and to burn out, and we believe that when a story brings you back to the basics and back to why you started writing in the first place, it's something special.

Of course, every book has a team behind it. Thank you to AP Fuchs who was there when this concept was born and who encouraged us to take this idea and turn it into a story. Thank you also for the top-notch editing and cover design.

Sincere appreciation to Jessica Gollub for taking our promotional photos, which meant tolerating these awkward authors turned not-so-super models.

To the Creators Retreat people—Greg, Chad, Andrew, Brenden, Adam, Josh—thank you for the friendly competition and for pushing us to finish the first draft.

Thanks to our cheerleaders, Rebekah, Andrew, Elissa, Heather, Kyle, and Adam. Thanks to the Anita Factor writers' group—Christina, Gabe, Jodi, Larry, MaryLou, Melanie, Pat, and Suzanne.

And last, but not least, we'd like to thank our families for their ongoing support.

Melinda Marshall

Melinda Marshall writes novels for teens and adults, and she writes short stories. Her award nominated first book, *Enslavement*, written under pen name, Melinda Friesen, is book one in the YA dystopian *One Bright Future* series. The second book in the series, *Subversion*, was released in September of 2016. *The High-Maintenance Ladies of the Zombie Apocalypse* is her third book. She lives in Winnipeg with her family. Learn more about her and her books at www.melindafriesen.com.

Links:
Instagram: @melindafriesen
Twitter: @melindafriesen
Facebook: @melindafriesen1

Christine Steendam

Christine Steendam is the award-winning author of the Great Canadian Plains Series and the Ocean Series. She also flirts with sci-fi and comic book writing. Christine makes her home in Manitoba, Canada on a sprawling 15 acre ranch with her husband, two young sons, and a brood of animals.

www.christinesteendam.com
kcsteendam@gmail.com

Other books by Christine Steendam
Owned by the Ocean
Heart Like an Ocean
Betrayed by the Ocean
Unforgiving Plains
Ropes & Reins
Shadows of the Unseen